FOR THE LOVE OF CHLOE

WENDY SMITH

Photography by GOLDEN CZERMAK / FURIOUSFOTOG

Cover model COREY SQUIRES

Cover Design by MOSS BOOK COVERS

Edited by CREATING INK

This book is written in New Zealand English, and as such contains phrasing and kiwi colloquialisms.

ISBN-13: 978-1-991303-02-8

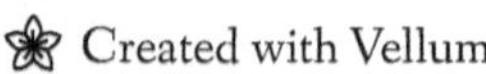

ONE
CHLOE

EVERY MUSCLE in my body aches.

And I really resent the fact that I'm the only one in my family who can drive.

"Mum, how much longer?"

It's Braden's turn riding shotgun, and I'm so over being asked that question that it takes everything in me not to stop the car and shove him out the door.

I love my son, but right now he and his brother are driving me insane.

"We're nearly there."

"You said that half an hour ago," Xander says from the back seat.

"I meant it then, and I mean it now. Don't make me go the long way."

"There's a long way?" He groans, slumping as much as the seatbelt will allow.

"I can make one."

Xander sighs.

"Why don't we drive past the new house on the way to Grandma's place?"

"Yes." Braden grins.

There's no answer from Xander, but he's probably ignoring me after our last exchange. Braden's the sweet, optimistic one. Xander's the moody, serious child. For identical twins, they're very different.

"It's just a small detour. Xander? What do you think?"

"Whatever."

I roll my eyes and take the next turn, heading toward the house. My heart pounds as we grow closer. This house means a lot to me, and I'm sure my boys will love it too. But it's hard making a fresh start, even if I am back in my home town.

It takes a few more minutes, but I slow as I approach and pull up outside our new home.

"Is this it?" Xander asks.

I bite my inner cheek. "No. I just thought I'd stop at some random house to prank you even though I'm exhausted and want to collapse into bed."

He shoots me the side-eye. "So ... this is it."

"Xander Cooper, you've seen the photos. You're smarter than this."

"I'm not sure about that." Braden ruffles his twin brother's hair, and Xander slaps his arm with a laugh.

"Let's go to your grandmother's. She'll be excited to see you two."

"Can't we stay here?" Xander asks.

I sigh. "We could, but there are beds at her place, and I can get some sleep without having to find the linen and make our beds. Plus, she'll have food."

"I'm hungry," Braden says.

"Of course you are." I smile. "We'll come back in the morning and start unpacking."

"This is the house Dad wanted, right?" Xander asks.

A lump forms in my throat. "Uh-huh."

"Why this house?"

"Catch up, Chloe."

Scott cycles faster than I do. School starts in half an hour, and as usual, I'm lagging behind.

He stops by the side of the road to wait for me.

"Slow down." I moan as I pull up beside him.

He grins. "Do you know why I stopped here?"

"No. Why?" He's up to something. There's that cheeky grin on his face that I adore.

"One day, I'm going to buy this house." He points and I look at the white, two storey, Victorian-style house.

"What are you talking about?"

"One day we'll come back here and raise our family, Chlo. And this house is so us. There's a swimming pool and everything."

I look back at the house. It's got a basic front garden, and I can't see anything behind it.

"How do you know?"

"My mum was the agent. She just sold it."

I laugh. "So what makes you think it'll ever go up for sale again?"

He shrugs. "Because it's our dream home. And I plan on making all your dreams come true."

Leaning over as far as my bike will allow, I plant a kiss on his lips. He grabs my arm to steady us, and I laugh despite his lips being on mine.

"Get a room, you guys." Hunter Emerson flies past us on his bike.

"Let's see if we can beat him to school," Scott says.

I laugh as he takes off, shaking my head while I move at my own speed.

"Mum? Why this house?" Braden asks.

"Your dad thought it was perfect for raising a family. And I need all the space I can get with two sixteen-year-olds as big as you two are."

Xan laughs. "I can't wait to see inside."

For a moment, I'm tempted to take them in, but my aching back reminds me that I have an appointment with an already made bed at Mum's.

"We'll be back in the morning. Then you can move into your rooms and make them your own."

"Can we stop for takeaways on the way to Gran's place?"

I shake my head. "She's cooking dinner for us. Let's get going because I really need to stretch my legs."

"Thanks for bringing us past here, Mum," Braden says.

"You're welcome. Tomorrow we'll make it all our own."

"I wish Dad was here to see it."

I play with my bottom lip between my teeth. "So do I, honey. So do I."

IT'S BEEN a long time since I've been home.

Scott and I managed to get through teenage parenthood while he qualified as a lawyer, and then we went to the UK for the first few years before coming back to New Zealand.

I flew back to Napier a couple of times with the boys, but when we returned, we settled into a life in Auckland and didn't really travel a lot after that.

And then we lost Scott.

It's bittersweet being here. This is the house where we spent hours hanging out together when we were kids, and where he'd sneak over to see me when we were teenagers. He kissed me for the first time in this yard.

Not having him here with us is cruel.

I blow out a long breath to stop myself from tearing up as I stop the car.

"This is it. This is where I grew up," I say.

"It's so small. Did you really live here?" Braden asks.

I laugh. "I did. It was just Mum, Dad, and your Uncle Caleb. It's a three-bedroom house. You've been spoiled."

"I'm just glad we've got a big house. And a pool. I can't wait to go for a swim."

"I've got no idea what condition the pool is in, so that might have to wait a while."

He rolls his eyes, and I shake my head.

Mum appears at the back door. Her smile warms my heart and makes me feel even more at home.

I unclick my seatbelt, open the door and step out of the car.

"Chloe." Mum practically skates across the yard, her eyes wide, and I all but fall into her arms—it's so good to be home. "How was the drive?"

"Long. I'm exhausted. I just want to sleep."

She kisses me on the forehead. "The beds are made. You've got your own room, and the boys are together if that's okay."

"Probably not, but it's only one night so they'll have to deal with it." I laugh.

Her gaze shifts to Braden and Xander, who are now standing behind me. "Oh, it's so good to see you two." Mum's head tilts back a little. "You've grown so much."

She lets go of me, and both boys step forward to hug her, my mother disappearing in their arms as they dwarf her tiny frame. I smile, knowing how she feels right now; the boys take after their father in height, not me.

They're so much like him, and it makes my heart ache.

Mum looks like a pig in mud, she's so happy to see them both. I'm glad we came here for the night so she could see them before we spend however long unpacking.

"Come in, all of you. I've cooked a lamb roast with all the trimmings. I'm sure you're all hungry."

I nod, despite knowing the lamb will be dryer than the Sahara. My mum's never been the best cook. But I appreciate the effort more than I can say.

Dad is just inside the door, and he hugs me tight as the others walk past us and into the kitchen.

"It's good to see you, love. Drive okay?"

I nod. "Just long."

"Caleb passes on his regards. He had other plans for the night, but he'll come and visit you at the new house."

I bite down my smirk. If I know my brother at all, his regards will involve the words 'fuck you.' He loves me, really, but he never stops giving me a hard time. It helps me keep sane, even at a distance.

"Thanks, Dad. I'm sure we'll catch up soon. He'll be 'round once the swimming pool is up and running."

Dad chuckles. "No doubt."

"Well, if everyone gets washed up, I'll serve dinner. Boys, go wash your hands."

I catch Xander and Braden's gazes. "Come on, you two. Let's get cleaned up."

I'd kill for a shower, but my stomach grumbles and reminds me that I refused to stop for food earlier. The drive is long enough without extending it.

By the time we get back to the table, Mum's put the food out, and I breathe in the familiar smell of her cooking. It's not that great, but right now I'd eat a horse and the rider if I had to.

Dad carves the roast, and we pile our plates high with food.

"Gravy?" Mum asks.

My boys both shake their heads while I roll my eyes at them.

"You should have the gravy," I say.

"Muuum." Braden moans. He's not usually a whiner, but it's been a big week of packing and moving and we'll all be happy to be settled.

"Trust me. You should have the gravy." It's the only moisture the meat's going to get, and Xander at least picks up my suggestion and takes the offered gravy boat from his grandmother. Braden follows suit, exchanging a glance with his brother.

But regardless of how dry it is, we all plough into it and eat until we're full. I lean back in my seat and let out a loud burp.

"Mum." Xander laughs. He's such a moody kid that it does my heart good to hear it.

"Pardon me. Thanks, Mum."

My mother laughs. "You're welcome. Do you want dessert? I've got ice cream."

"The boys might. I'm fine. I'll make a coffee."

I get up and take my plate to the kitchen, placing it in the dishwasher before turning on the jug.

For a moment, I look out the window to the backyard.

"What are you doing?" I laugh.

"You know I like you, Chloe. Don't you?" He's so goofy when he's nervous. I don't even know why he is. We've been friends since we were little kids.

"I like you too."

Scott leans in and pecks me on the lips. I blush and turn my head. But it seals the deal. I'm thirteen years old and Scott Cooper's girlfriend.

I'm pretty sure this makes it official.

"Mum?"

I blink and turn my head to see Braden frowning, head tilted, nose scrunched, biting a thumbnail.

"Yes? Hello."

"Xander and I are going to unpack the car after dessert. Do you want us to bring in your things?"

I nod. "Sure. That'd be great. Thank you."

"Are you okay?"

I smile, and nod again. "I'm fine. Just tired. It's been a long day. Both of you need to learn to drive."

"Does that mean you're buying us a car?" Xander asks.

I laugh. "Maybe I'll make you drive me around in mine."

His face falls, but I already have plans to do just that when the time is right. It won't be anything too pricey, but Scott and I talked about it before his death and planned to make sure whatever we bought, or they bought, was safe.

Although, if I could make it so, neither of them will ever be on the road.

"We'll talk about it when the time is right."

I make my coffee and take it to the living room where I can sit in peace for a while and drink it. I'm in such a weird space right now. It's been four years since my husband died, but this is the biggest move I've made so far to start a new life. But no matter where I go, he's there too.

I close my eyes. It doesn't matter how long it's been since I was last in this house, but it's home. And I'm glad I'm here for the night before we start the new chapter in our lives.

Being here eases the fear of it all.

WITH OUR THINGS OUT of the car and the boys in their room, I head to bed.

I close the door behind me and face plant into the rock hard mattress. But I don't care.

Standing, I drop my jeans to the floor and unhook my bra, pulling it off underneath my T-shirt. And then I flop back onto the bed and pull the blanket over me.

The last few weeks have been exhausting.

There was no real plan to move back here. Scott and I had talked about it in a vague sense, and we'd kept an eye on the property market for years. Seeing the house come up for sale had seemed like too good an opportunity to miss.

It seemed like fate.

His life insurance payment was sitting in the bank just gathering interest, so I got to pocket the profit from our Auckland house as well as not having to worry about a mortgage here.

I'd swap it all for having him back in a heartbeat.

But, that's not an option. I made my decision, and the boys were surprisingly happy to go along with it. I thought I'd have more of a fight, but they were also struggling with the constant reminders of their father.

This is a fresh start for all three of us.

I can't wait to get back to my own bed, but for the meantime, I'm going to sleep like Braden did when he was a baby—for a long stretch of time.

It doesn't take long to drift off, despite the hardness of the mattress and the pillow being too soft.

Nothing really matters right now.

"Mum?"

I've been a light sleeper since the day those boys were born, and I smile to myself through my sleepy haze.

"Braden."

He pulls the blanket up and slides into bed with me. "I hate sharing rooms with Xander."

"It's only for one night, honey."

He snuggles in against me. "Grandma can't cook either. Dinner was awful."

I chuckle. "I know. I did try to tell you."

"You're cooking tomorrow night, right?"

I roll over, slide my arm under his neck and press a kiss to his forehead. "It's our first night in the house. Maybe we can order pizza."

"I like that idea."

The bed sinks behind me, and I shake my head. "Hello, Xander."

"Grandma's cooking sucks."

All I can do is laugh.

"Mum said we can get pizza tomorrow, Xan."

"Thank God."

"Can we all just get some sleep?" I pull my arm out from under Braden and roll onto my back.

When they were little, the boys would always climb into bed between Scott and me. They insisted they'd grown out of it by the time they were nine. But since his death, they do it when they need reassurance. And it's never just one. It's always both of them.

Me? I still hate this mattress, but tomorrow I'll be back in my soft, king size bed. I'm too tired to even care that we're squished into this double.

We're home.

TWO
CHLOE

MY EYEBALLS ACHE.

Maybe I should have stayed in the new house—linen or not. Sleeping in a too small bed with two nearly-adult-teenagers wasn't the brightest thing I've ever done, but I was so tired last night, I didn't care.

My back hurts right along with my eyes.

"Did you have a good sleep?" Mum asks, as I stagger out into the kitchen blurry eyed and almost as tired as the night before.

"It was fine, Mum. I'm just looking forward to sleeping in my own bed tonight."

She smiles. "I'm sure. I've packed some sandwiches for your lunch so you can focus on getting unpacked and not have to worry."

"Thank you." I am grateful for what my family have done for me. My brother took over this end of the move to help me out, and being able to come right here was a relief last night, even if I have to stifle a yawn.

"Take a seat and I'll make you a coffee."

My boys sit at the table with two steaming mugs of hot chocolate and bowls I assume had cereal in them.

"Good morning," I say.

"Morning, Mum." Braden smiles.

Xander scrapes the bottom of his bowl. "Can we go now?"

I know he's keen to get to the new house and shut the rest of the world out. It's his thing.

"I'll just drink my coffee and we'll get going. Grandma's made us some lunch."

Braden's eyes widen, but he looks back down at his hot chocolate.

"Did you want anything to eat, Chloe?" Mum asks.

I shake my head. "No, I'll just have the coffee and get going."

She places it in front of me. "Are you sure? I have cereal, and I have toast."

"I'm sure. Thanks, Mum."

"You always did eat like a sparrow. No wonder you're so thin."

I swallow down any smart remark. I've never been a huge eater, but I've also had a lot of stress to deal with, and moving hasn't helped.

Besides, I'm as keen as Xander to get to the new house now.

"I'm just tired, Mum. That bed hasn't got any more comfortable over time." I laugh.

"You're not wrong," Braden grumbles.

I sip my coffee while Mum and Dad make small talk with the boys. My brain's so frazzled, I'm not sure I'll get much done other than unpack a few things and crawl into bed.

After a while, I smile and drain my coffee.

"Right. Finish your drinks and let's go. We have a lot to do today."

"Did you want to come back for dinner?" Mum says.

I shake my head. "I promised the boys we could have pizza tonight. It's been a tiring few days, so I think we deserve a treat."

She nods. "Just let me know if you need anything more."

"I will. Thank you for everything."

I BREATHE in the warm air gently blowing in through the open car window and smile as we make our way to our new home.

"Is this the way we came last night?" Xander's confusion is clear in his voice.

"Not quite. I'm just going to grab some milk and bread so we have some basic food in the house."

"So we don't have to eat Grandma's lunch?" Braden asks.

I laugh. "She made sandwiches, and if I know her there'll be peanut butter, and vegemite. She knows I like them."

"Together?" He stares at me with wide eyes.

"No. She's not that bad." I roll my eyes and pull over at the side of the road beside a dairy. "Do you two want anything else?"

"Can you see if they've got hot pies? I'm still hungry after breakfast," Xander asks.

I chuckle. "Sure. Is that for both of you?"

"Yes, please." Braden adds.

Tomorrow, I'll have to go to the supermarket. Living with two sixteen-year-olds who are bottomless pits when it comes to food isn't cheap, but it's one more step to settling into a normal life here.

"Okay. I'll be back in a minute."

I grab my bag from the backseat and head into the dairy. Grabbing milk, bread, and hot pies, I head back out to the car. The food smells so good, my stomach rumbles.

"Can we eat them now?"

I laugh. "Yes, and I got one for me too."

"Maybe then you won't be so thin." Braden does an impersonation of his grandmother that's so accurate, and I just shake my head.

"Don't do that." I moan.

"She shouldn't be so mean."

"She's my mother, and she worries about me." I take a bite of my pie. "Oh, my God. That's so good."

Xander nods. "Better than dinner last night."

I grin. "She tries. Don't be too hard on her. She's very happy to have you home." Pausing, I take another bite and swallow it down. "We still have your other grandparents to go and visit."

"Do we have to?" Braden asks.

I try not to sigh too loudly. My relationship with my mother-in-law is strained. It was fine when we were kids, but my teenage pregnancy didn't go down well at all, and of course her beloved boy wasn't as much to blame as me.

But she does love the boys.

We did our best to shelter them from any resentment she had toward me. Scott made it clear that he didn't appreciate it, and always took my side. Sadly, my sweet boys worked it all out for themselves. And when she showed up for Scott's funeral and tried to take over, ignoring his wishes, it set her on a whole new path of disliking me.

I'm not looking forward to seeing her.

We eat in silence before I start the car and set off again.

My beautiful new home, with the veranda running around the outside, and the sweet little garden. It's a sight for sore eyes, even after our brief visit yesterday. It's a connection to the past and all the love I had back then. A love I miss so much.

I pull into the driveway and come to a stop, and Braden and Xander are out the car before I can even catch a breath.

"Mum, hurry up."

I'm not even sure which one it is who calls out, but I sigh and switch off the car before opening the door and stepping out.

It's not a long walk to the front door, and my hand shakes as I slide the key in the lock and turn the handle.

Buying a house was the biggest thing I've ever done by myself, and it scared the hell out of me. But I think it's one more way of me claiming a new life, and I'm proud I did it. The boys were a little unsure at first—they had friends back in Auckland—but in the end they agreed it was a good decision for our family.

They'll keep touch with those friends, and we have plenty of room for them to visit.

"Wow. It's bigger than I thought it was," Braden says.

I step into the entranceway and look around. Of course I've seen pictures, but this is so much better. To my right, polished wooden floor gives way to thick carpet in the living room, and carpeted stairs lead up to the bedrooms with the kitchen and dining down the back of the house.

It's clean, and fresh, and home.

"Take your shoes off and go and explore. The beds should already be in our rooms. I just have to find the box of linen. Hopefully your uncle got the movers to put it in a sensible place." I laugh.

Both of them rush past me and up the stairs. My head thumps from last night's bad sleep, so my goal today is to make the beds and unpack enough of the kitchen that I can make a coffee.

If he did as I asked, Caleb had the movers put the boxes in the rooms they were destined for. I made sure they were clearly marked—he just had to do his part.

As I walk into the kitchen, I breathe a sigh of relief when I spot the important kitchen supplies box on the bench as requested.

Tearing it open, I pull out my kettle and the coffee making supplies.

The box also contains four mugs, and I grab them out and give them a quick wash in the sink before filling the kettle and plugging it in.

It'll take a few minutes, and I lean against the bench and close my eyes.

"Hey, sis."

I turn.

My older brother, Caleb, stands in the doorway, a wide smile on his face. He's probably the one person I kept in touch with the most back home. He even visited us when we were overseas. And the boys adore him.

I'm glad they'll have his influence while we're living here, even if he's forty and still single.

There are no words that can describe how I feel about seeing him here. My heart's overwhelmed by his presence, and I say nothing but cross the room and throw myself into his arms.

He chuckles and kisses the top of my head. "I'm guessing you're glad to see me?"

"I'm tired and you're such a sight for sore eyes. Thank you for organising this end of the move for me."

"You're welcome. How was your drive?"

I pull back and nod. "Long. Want a coffee?"

"I'd love one. Where are the boys?"

"Upstairs, unpacking in their rooms. I still have to make the beds and haven't progressed past the kitchen yet, but I'm just looking forward to sleeping in my own bed tonight."

He nods. "You stayed in that rock hard bed at Mum's last night?"

"Yes, with a teenager on either side. But I have plans for pizza and an early night tonight."

"Sounds like a good idea."

I let him go and return to the bench to line up another mug.

"I bet you're glad to be here," he says.

"I am. I'll be enrolling the boys in school tomorrow, and then we can get some routine back in our lives." I sigh. "After all this unpacking."

The kettle flicks off, and I spoon the coffee and sugar into the cups before pouring the milk and then the hot water.

He's sitting at the kitchen table and smiles as I approach.

"And what about you? All I've heard these past weeks is how important this move was for the boys, but do you get a life of your own now?"

I shrug, placing his coffee in front of him and sitting opposite. "I get to come home and spend more time with you."

"Stop it." He laughs. "You deserve some happiness. Lord knows you've been through enough. It's been four years."

I take a sip of coffee to avoid speaking straight away. "I'm not sure there's a set amount of time for grieving."

He leans forward. "Of course not. But you're so young and you have a whole new life ahead of you. I know you wanted more kids. You could still have that."

I know he's right. And I have had offers. But when you lose the love of your life at thirty-one, that's a mighty big gap to fill.

Tears prick my eyes. What I need is to go and sort out my bed and have a sleep—not be preached at by my brother. "It's not just me I have to worry about."

"The boys will be fine. They're old enough to understand you finding someone new. I'd volunteer to babysit while you're on dates, but they don't need me."

I laugh at the thought of Caleb taking care of my near-adult boys.

He fixes his blue-eyed gaze on me. I love my brother with all my heart, but right now I want to smack him even though, I'm sure, this is all stuff I need to hear.

"Find someone who loves you with their whole heart, Chloe. Scott's not the only one who'll do that. You might be my annoying little sister, but I know you're so full of love, and when the right person comes along, you'll be able to share that again."

I blink back tears and chew on my bottom lip. "When did you get so soppy?"

"I'm in love. Again. But that's beside the point."

I laugh. "You're in love?"

"Yes, and it's real this time. Not like all the other times."

Nodding, I wipe the tears from my face and smile. "Then, I'm happy for you. When can I meet her?"

"Well, we've only been out once, so not just yet." He flashes that grin at me, and all I can do is laugh again. Caleb and I have always been polar opposites. He's never done anything but play the field whereas I've been with just one person for all of my teens right up until death did us part. "That's better. At least you're smiling. Anyway, just so you know, I treated the pool when I was here the other day and got the pump up and running so you can go for a swim. There was a cover left on it, so it wasn't too bad. It should be good when you want to use it."

"Thank you."

He takes a long drink of his coffee. "I bet you can't wait to set up your coffee machine."

My eyebrows rise. "Is that you criticising my coffee making skills?"

He laughs. "No, but when it is set up, I'll know where to come for a good, free one."

I shake my head at him. "You know you're welcome any time. Even if it is just for my coffee."

"Uncle Caleb." Braden comes bursting into the room.

"Hey, buddy. How's it going?"

"Good. We're having pizza for dinner tonight. Can you join us?"

Caleb exchanges a glance with me. "Not tonight, but I will soon."

Braden's face falls.

"Sometime during the week I'll swing by and take you guys for a drive. Give your mum a bit of time by herself. Maybe we can go and grab some lunch together. Sound good?"

Braden nods. "That'd be great."

"Is everything where it's meant to be? I followed your instructions." Caleb shifts his gaze to me.

I nod. "Seems to be. No one's complained yet."

He smiles. "That's good."

Braden heads to the bench and opens the lid on the box of sandwiches Mum gave us.

"Can we eat these?"

"It's not even lunchtime," I say.

"But I'm hungry."

Caleb laughs. "I bet you're always hungry."

"Pretty much." I stand and pick up the box, placing it in the middle of the table. "Help yourself and tell your brother he can as well. I'm sure unpacking uses a lot of energy."

Braden grabs a handful of food and disappears back upstairs.

"They are so much like me when I was their age," Caleb says.

"I hope not." I poke my tongue at him.

He drains his coffee and stands. "Anyway, I just wanted to make sure you got here okay. I'll pop in during the week and take those boys off your hands for a while."

"Thank you. I seem to be saying that a lot to you lately. I'll walk you out."

I walk around the table and hug him again. As much as we used to snark at each other, he really is one of the best parts of being home.

Following him out to the front door, I stop as he opens it.

"Hey, the school reunion's on Saturday. Are you going?"

I shrug. "I registered, but I'll see how I feel by then."

"It's three days away, so at least you'll have had some sleep. You should go. It'll do you some good." He laughs.

"What about you? Are you going?"

Caleb screws up his face. "It depends. I'm going out on Saturday with my new lady, so if that goes well, no. If it goes badly, then I might see you there."

I roll my eyes. "You're terrible."

"Yeah, but you love me. Call me if you need any help with anything."

"I will. Thanks again."

For a moment, I watch him as he walks down the front path to his car. He's always lived such a carefree life, but he's been there when I needed him. He drove through the night to be with me when Scott died, and back then he did take care of my boys.

I owe my brother a great debt.

And maybe I'll take his advice.

AFTER CLEARING AWAY THE CUPS, I walk to the base of the stairs and sigh.

Reaching the boys' bedrooms, I smile as I turn my head left and then right to see them busy, setting up their rooms. Xander's even making his bed.

"You found the linen box, then?" I ask.

"Go and look in your room, Mum," Braden calls out.

I walk to the end of the hallway and into my bedroom. There are boxes everywhere, but against one wall, my bed is made. It's enough to bring tears to my eyes again.

"We raised them well, Scott," I whisper. "You'd be proud of them."

"Have a sleep, Mum. We'll unpack our stuff and we can order pizza later." Xander's voice comes from his room.

I smile. A nap will do me the world of good, and there's no time limit on unpacking. It can all wait until later.

Stripping down to just my T-shirt, I slide between the fresh sheets and sigh.

Lying down on one pillow, I pull the other pillow close and breathe into it. Scott's scent is long since gone, but sleeping in our old bed gives me a sense of peace.

Caleb means well, encouraging me to look for love, but I'm not in any hurry.

I'm not sure if lightning really does strike twice.

THREE

HUNTER

I HAVEN'T MET my new neighbour yet, but she has the nicest arse I've ever seen.

I'm a terrible man for ogling her out the window, but there's no other way for me to describe it as I watch her white bikini clad body clearing the leaves out of the pool.

She bends over, completely oblivious to me watching her, and I feel like such a dirty old man, but at the same time, I can't stop watching.

I didn't see her face—she's wearing a cap and sunglasses, but she's spent most of the time turned away from me anyway, the large scoop in hand, flinging the leaves over the pool fence and onto the lawn.

My phone rings loudly from the other side of the room, and I sigh, walking over to pick it up and returning to my spot by the window. I glance at the screen before answering.

"Darren."

"Hunter."

Darren's an old school buddy and client of my security firm. He's nice enough, but I've been resisting the invites he and his wife keep extending for dinner.

"I'm calling to check if you're still coming to the school reunion."

I pull back the blind, one eye still on the woman next door. The previous occupants of that house already caused me enough trouble. I don't need any more.

"Not really sure if I can be bothered. I already see the people who actually mean something to me on a semi-regular basis."

"And the rest of the time, you're a recluse. Maybe it's time to get back on the horse."

I snort. "I rode enough horses after my marriage break-up."

"What if I had a big incentive for you to make the effort?" There's a teasing tone in his voice.

The woman next door drops the scoop on the ground and dives into the pool. I'm not sure there's anything that could incentivise me to go to the school reunion with the view from here.

"Like what?"

"Meredith dropped off some baking for the fundraising table. She saw the name tags and there's one for Chloe Cooper."

I swivel my gaze away from the window, turning back toward my bed. "Really?"

"Yes. And more interestingly, not one for Scott. Just Chloe."

I draw in a sharp breath. Chloe Cooper was my one who got away. But not really. She was Chloe Baxter back then, and utterly, hopelessly in love with Scott. He loved her, too, and I was just his best friend with a crush on the girl I couldn't have.

For nearly three years I kept it to myself, but when Scott worked it out, he dropped me like a hot potato and banished me from his life. They left town to go to university shortly afterward and never kept in touch. I always wondered how much Chloe knew.

"Guess I'm coming to this reunion, then."

Darren laughs. "I thought that might change your mind."

"You know me too well."

After I've disconnected the call, I sit on the side of my bed.

Chloe Cooper.

Even though I haven't seen her in years, the thought of her brings a smile to my lips.

She might not have been mine, but she was often the sunshine that helped get me through some really rough times as a teen. There wasn't a day when she didn't have a smile on her face, and she listened to me complain as my parents' marriage fell apart.

Chloe was my friend, but she came to mean more to me than that. And of all the people I went to school with, Chloe and Scott are the two I missed.

It's time to build some bridges.

"HE'S IN YOUR OFFICE," my PA, Liz, says as I walk in the door. I work from home when I can but come in for important meetings like this.

One I can't avoid.

Gary's sitting on the couch in my office and rises when I walk in the door. I wave him to sit down. We've been here too many times before.

I drop my jacket on the back of my chair and take a seat by the couch.

"Hunter, I'm sorry."

I swallow hard. Last night I had to juggle my workers to cover the shift that Gary missed because he went out drinking instead. To get the call at some crazy hour that he hadn't turned up was concerning. To find he wasn't far from the property he was supposed to be patrolling was infuriating.

"I told you last time that I wouldn't tolerate this. I've tried to be supportive. What else should I be doing? Tell me."

His sheepish expression doesn't help. He knows what he did was wrong, but he's been struggling with alcoholism for months and hasn't sought help despite me having to haul him in for warnings all the way through.

His performance has been subpar for a long time, and I'm at the end of my rope. I only employ the best, and he's good at his job when he's not drinking.

Right now, he's so far from that it's tearing me apart.

"You need to get help. We've had this conversation before. I'll pay your full wages while you go through rehab, but we can't go on the way we are."

He nods. "I know."

"I can't force you to do it, but I can't continue like this. We're way past second chances and giving you a fair go. I've done that. I've bent over backward to try to get you the help you need." I take a deep breath. "Legally, the next step is to fire you, and I don't want that, but you're leaving me with no choice. Is that what you want?"

He shakes his head. "I'm trying."

"Call the number I gave you and get the help you need. It's the only option you have left."

I can't fold. If I keep sending him on jobs he doesn't turn up to, it's my business that suffers. He's leaving me very little choice other than to fire him, and while I have a reputation for being tough, I'm not completely heartless.

"This is literally destroying your life."

He hangs his head. "I know it is."

"The only person who can turn this around is you. Get some help."

I sigh in frustration as he leaves. He's not a bad person, just someone struggling with addiction. But there's a line I have to draw.

He gives me a nod. "Thanks, Hunter."

As he makes his way out of the office, I follow, stopping in the doorway.

"Do you think he'll do it?" Liz asks.

I shrug. "Who knows? I hope so. He's a smart kid, but this alcohol thing is dragging him down."

"Hunter, you've done everything you can to avoid firing him, but if he doesn't sort this out ..."

Nodding, I head toward the door. I need some fresh air after that.

"Are you going home?" she asks.

"Yes. I'll be on mobile if you want me."

"Have a good day."

The sun is so warm on my face, and for a fleeting moment, my mind wanders to the woman in the pool next door. How good would that be right now? To swim in the cool water, relax in the sunshine and forget about my worries.

Truth be known, I'm a little envious

I'll have to settle for a walk in the park to cool down instead.

FOUR

CHLOE

"I'VE GOT IT."

Xander squeezes past me as the broadband technician packs up his things. He's carrying the router and a bunch of cables, and for the millionth time I'm thankful he and his brother are good at the technical stuff.

They both hate that we had to wait until today to get fibre installed, but now it's in, we'll all be able to get on with our online lives.

At least it gives them something to do tonight while I head out to this reunion.

I've spent the past few days tossing up whether or not to go. But now I'm not feeling tired, and it would do me good to be around people again. Besides, I can always use the boys as an excuse to leave early if I have to.

"Mum, where's your laptop?" Xander asks.

"It's on the table. Why?"

"We just want to make sure it's all working before the tech leaves."

I hold up my palms. "Do whatever you have to do."

He runs to the table, and I smile. I know both him and his brother are anxious to get back online and chat with their friends. I can write without the net, but I use my social media to sell books, and it's so much easier to use a computer than my phone.

"It all looks good. Speed test is fast. This is better than the internet we had in the old house."

I nod. "I got a faster plan."

He beams. I don't even care if this means he's more antisocial while home as long as he's smiling. It's a rare thing to see with Xander.

"Thanks, Mum."

"I'm glad you're happy, honey."

I watch him show the broadband technician out, and then instead of heading straight upstairs, he returns and gives me an unexpected hug. I close my eyes, wrap my arms around his chest and enjoy it while it lasts.

"I know it's been hard, Mum, but I think we made the right choice."

"Me too," I whisper. I'm not sure if he realises what this show of affection means to me.

We seem to stand there for the longest time, but I don't mind at all. Xander's heart is big but guarded, and I'm making the most of this.

"You have to get ready to go out."

I grin. I wouldn't call him clingy, but he hasn't been at all receptive to me having much of a social life. He likes to know where I am, and I know he has his reasons.

"Maybe. Maybe I'll stay home and hang out with you."

I pull back and laugh at the pained expression on his face. I can't imagine anything worse for a teenage boy when his mother wants to spend time with him.

"Don't you need to have a shower or something?" He turns and walks toward the door.

"Are you saying I smell?" I call out. His fading laughter is music to my ears.

But he's right. Time is marching on, and it's not like those two will be any kind of company tonight. I'll lose my boys to their bedrooms while they play computer games and hang out with their friends online.

Sure enough, by the time I reach the top of the stairs, both bedroom doors are closed.

At least they're happy.

I CLOSE my eyes as the shower water hits my face.

It's been a while since I put much effort into going out, but tonight should be fun.

Lathering up the body wash, I rinse myself off and shampoo my hair.

The longer I spend getting ready, the more I'm looking forward to mingling with people my own age.

And people who used to know me.

A lot has happened in my life since I last saw any of them, but I can't forget that it's been a lot of years and so much will have happened to them too.

I turn off the shower, and step out, grabbing a large towel to wrap around myself.

Wiping the fogged up bathroom mirror, I brush some wet tendrils off my face and then reach for the hairdryer in the cupboard below.

Cutting my hair was almost an act of defiance against grief. For years it hung to my waist, and even when I had the boys, I'd tie it up rather than cut it, even if they dug their little fingers in and twisted. But six months into widowhood, I wanted a change and had it cut into a bob.

I still miss the length sometimes, but days like this when I can dry it fast change my mind pretty quickly about growing it again.

My hands shake a little while I apply makeup. I was never that great at it, but I manage to get it on evenly and smile at the change in me.

It makes me look younger and yet more mature all at once. I can live with that.

This feels like a huge amount of effort for one night out. Part of me just wants to order pizza and spend the night on the couch in front of the television, but I need to step out of my comfort zone.

The next step is working out what to wear. I guess I should have done this earlier in the day, but I've never been that organised. My wardrobe is full after unpacking my clothes a couple of days ago.

I've been out on the odd night with friends before, but this is my first solo outing. Maybe I should have hassled Caleb to take me, then again if I take my own car, I've got a way to leave if I need to.

Settling on a simple black cocktail dress, I tug off my towel and slip on my underwear before pulling the dress over my head.

Standing in front of the full-length mirror, I smooth the dress down and take a look at myself.

Who am I?

I haven't had my own identity in a long time. Scott's girlfriend, Braden and Xander's mother, Scott's wife, Scott's widow. They're all me, but I can't remember the last time I was just Chloe.

I'll still be all those things, but it's time to claim *me* back.

I don't even really look like me right now. I've always been the jeans and T-shirt kind of girl, but that changed when I became the wife of an up-and-coming lawyer. This dress is from that time, and I look damn good in it even if I do say so myself.

My engagement ring glitters in the mirror, and I raise my hand to see it and the matching wedding ring still sitting on my finger.

For four years, I've kept wearing them, an indication to the world that I'm taken. If I were a braver woman, I'd take them off. But tonight, when this is an event we should have attended together, it gives me more confidence to leave them on.

It's not time to take them off yet, but it is time to get going.

VOICES COMING from the kitchen tell me where the boys are, and I venture in before I go to say goodbye.

"You look amazing, Mum," Braden says.

I smile and cup his cheek. "Thank you."

"You don't even look old." He laughs.

I look at him in mock horror. I'm sure I'm ancient to him.

"Braden, don't be mean to Mum. Maybe one day she'll tell us what it was like to live with dinosaurs."

Gaping at Xander, I fight the urge to smile as he grins at me.

"I'm kidding. Some of my friends think you're a MILF, but that's just gross. You're my mum," Braden says.

I clamp my lips together to try and stop myself from laughing, but tears prick my eyes because I'm trying so hard.

Giving him a hug, I let it go and laugh out loud. "I love you, Braden Cooper. But that acronym is never coming out of your mouth again."

He shrugs. "That's fine with me."

Still chuckling, I pick up my purse and head toward the door. "Be good," I call. "There's some money on the fridge in case you want to order takeaways. I won't be late. Love you."

I'm sure one of them is on the phone to the pizza place before I even make it outside.

Smiling all the way to my car, I get in and take a deep breath. Here goes nothing. I could make my way here blindfolded, and I'm soon arriving at the gates of the school.

My stomach churns, but I ignore it.

I haven't been back here for years, but nothing seems to have changed.

The buildings look freshly painted, but they're still the old blocks of classrooms that existed when I was here.

It's obvious where the reunion function's being held because the hall is all lit up, and music carries through the air.

We never meant to turn our back on our home town. Our lives just took us in a different direction, and we went with it. When all you need is each other, nothing else really matters.

It should have. Then I wouldn't have the mixed emotions I do now.

I pull into the car park and find an empty spot. For a moment, I clutch the steering wheel before turning the engine off.

Being here alone is weird.

But I have to push myself through the memories that dog me, and face up to the past before I can find my future.

I take a deep breath, grab my bag, open the door, and step out of the car.

It's time.

FIVE

HUNTER

I HATE BEING SOCIAL.

When my marriage to Piper broke up, I buried myself in other women. Nothing serious, but it wore thin after a while, and I haven't been big on socialising ever since.

This reunion is my idea of Hell, and there's only one reason I'm here.

So far, it seems like everyone's arrived except for Chloe, but I verified for myself that her name badge was at the door.

"Well, look who's here."

I turn to see Darren walking toward me, a smug expression on his face.

"Hi."

He extends his hand, and I shake it, not dropping my gaze. I know from his smug tone what he's getting at.

"I knew there was a big drawcard tonight. Still didn't know if it would bring you out. It's good to see you, man."

I nod. "Good to see you too."

"I gather she hasn't arrived yet?"

Huffing, I turn back to look at the entrance. "Not yet."

"Hunter, I know I've given you shit, but I know what she meant to you. I hope she does come, even if it's just to put a smile on that sour face."

I give him a gentle shove. "Hey."

"What you went through with Piper changed you. I just want my old friend back."

I meet his gaze. "I know you care. I'm fine."

He nods back past me. "There she is. I'm going to get another drink and leave you to it."

As he disappears into the distance, I catch my breath at the sight of *her* in the doorway.

There's no mistaking Chloe. Her blonde hair's cut shorter, into a wavy bob instead of hanging down her back like it used to. But that sun-kissed nose and her full lips still look the same as they did seventeen years ago.

God how I wanted to kiss those lips back then.

She fastens her name badge to her dress and looks around.

I can't take my eyes off her. She looks as good as she did when we were eighteen.

A smile lights up her face as our gazes meet, and she makes her way through the crowd until she's right in front of me.

My heart thuds.

"Hunter. It's been years. I'm so glad to see you."

I don't even get a word in before she wraps her arms around my waist and rests her head on my chest.

This is *so* unfair.

I wrap my arms around her and hug her tight. "Hey, Chlo. I'm glad to see you too. I was kinda surprised you were on the guest list."

She lets go. "Really? Why?"

"I haven't seen you since you left town. Didn't know if you'd be back for this."

She beams. "Well, I'm here. You look so good. When did you grow up?"

I chuckle. "Gee thanks."

"I just mean ... You were always taller than me, but I can't remember you being this tall."

I shrug. "I might have grown a few more inches. You look incredible. It's like all the years in between then and now never happened."

She draws in a deep breath as she lets me go. "Thank you. I know you're lying, but thank you."

"I wouldn't lie to you."

"One of my kids basically called me a dinosaur before I left the house. At least I know you're the same age as me." The cheeky grin she shares with me makes my whole body react.

"Oh my God. It's Chloe Baxter."

I suppress the urge to roll my eyes at the squeal that comes from behind us. Meredith appears and grabs Chloe's arms. Chloe shoots me a *what the fuck* look but smiles.

"Meredith."

"It's been forever."

Chloe nods. "It sure has. How are you?"

A crowd of our old school mates begin to gather around. Chloe will be the big curiosity here. Everyone else around us either left town and came back, or never left.

"I'm so good. My husband's around here somewhere. Do you remember Darren Carmichael?"

"I do."

"We got married a couple of years ago. We lived together forever before we got around to it. And we have three kids. Time's just flown by." She pauses. "What about you guys? Do you have kids?"

"Two boys," Chloe says.

There's tension in her face that wasn't there before, and it's got me curious. I'm not sure anyone else notices, but apart from Scott, I'm probably the person who knew Chloe best.

"And Scott. Where's he? Is he around here?"

Chloe blinks rapidly, and opens her mouth only to close it again without a word. She pulls away from Meredith and seems to struggle with the answer. I glare at Meredith. She's the one who alerted me to

Chloe coming here alone. Why do I get the feeling what she's asking is a loaded question?

"Chloe? Are you okay?" I ask.

Her brows knit, and she licks her lips, giving me a short nod.

Silence goes on for an eternity as she lets out a long breath and then chokes out the words. "Umm. I thought I'd handle this better. Scott died."

Her words crash into my brain, and for a moment I'm left unable to speak. How is that possible? I loved that guy like a brother until we fell out. How could I not know this?

"Oh, Chloe." Meredith touches her arm.

"I'm sorry. I need some fresh air." Tears well in Chloe's eyes, and she heads toward the nearest exit.

Meredith turns to me. "Did you know?"

"Of course I didn't fucking know. Excuse me."

I follow the path Chloe took until I reach the door and look around outside. The light is fading, but there's still enough for me to see her with her back to me. She's holding onto a fence, taking deep breaths.

"Chloe. Are you okay?"

She turns to look over her shoulder. "I'll be fine. I just haven't been asked that question for a long time."

"How long?" I draw up next to her. "How long has it been?"

"Four years." She shoots a glance at me. "I should handle it better by now, I guess."

I shake my head. "You loved him. I'm not sure these things are ever easy."

She looks at me longer this time. "Time helps, but it's still very hard."

"I bet." I reach over and rub her shoulder. "What brings you back to town? The reunion? Or is it something more permanent?"

"I'm back home for good." She sighs. "For a combination of reasons, but I want my boys to get to know this town and their grandparents. It was a tough decision, leaving everything they ever knew behind, but I think it'll be the right one."

I smile. "Well, I'm glad you're back in town anyway. I missed you."

"I missed you too. I'm glad you're here tonight. I don't know what possessed me to come here otherwise." She gives me a gentle laugh, and nudges my side. "What's your story?"

"Me?" I take a deep breath. "I'd kill for a drink right now, and I bet you would too."

Chloe nods. "That sounds like a wonderful idea."

"Do you want to go back inside, or do you want to get out of here?"

Her lips curl into a smile. "I should probably socialise. There are a lot of people I haven't seen in years."

I nudge her back with my elbow. "Yeah, but I'm more important than them."

Her smile widens. Seventeen years ago that would have made my heart sing, and I have to admit that, right now, my reaction isn't that different.

Chloe nods. "That's true. You are. Where are we going?"

"There's a quiet little pub on Hastings Street I go to from time to time. Do you need a ride?"

"I've got my car."

"No babysitters to rush home to?"

Chloe grins. "My babies are sixteen. They can look after themselves for one evening."

My mouth falls open. "No way. How is that even possible?"

"It's been a long time, Hunter. You lead and I'll follow in my car. One drink and something to eat because I'm starving."

"They do the best pub food."

"Sounds great."

"I'll grab my car and meet you at the car park entrance?"

She nods. "I'm the one driving the red Honda sedan. Not that you can probably see what colour it is in this light."

"I have a dark blue Ford Mustang."

Chloe wrinkles her nose. "Nice. You must be doing okay for yourself, then."

"Not too bad. See you in a minute?"

"Sure thing."

I head off to my car, smiling to myself.

Not in a million years did I imagine this scenario. But my mood darkens when I think of what she's just told me. Scott's dead. He was sometimes moody with a dark sense of humour, and Chloe was the light in his life. But we shared so much laughter, and until he realised how I felt about his girlfriend, we were close.

I need to know more.

THE SOUND she makes as she takes a big bite of a French fry makes my toes curl.

Everything's changed in both our lives, but this takes me back to when we used to hang out together, before Scott cut me out.

"These are so good. I'm glad we came here."

I smile. "Me too. The food's a lot better than the reunion would have been."

Chloe licks the salt from her fingers and takes a long sip of her beer. "I feel so bad for leaving, but I like this place better. And I get to catch up with the one person I actually wanted to see."

I chuckle. "Really?"

She puts her glass down. "When Scott died, we had the funeral in Auckland because all our friends were there. A part of me regrets not bringing him home. But that's what I'm doing now."

I frown. "What do you mean?"

"He was cremated, and he wanted me to make the decision about where to inter him. So, now I'm back, I need to work out when I'm ready to do that."

"Is there any hurry?"

She shakes her head. "For now I'm happy for him to be with me. I know that must sound weird."

I reach across the table and take her hand. "It sounds like you, and him, the two of you, had something really special."

She nods. "Right up until the end. But now I'm here, and it's taken a while, but I reached the point where I had to start thinking about myself and the boys rather than dwelling in the past." Chloe looks down at the table. "I still feel like, sometimes, I'm being selfish thinking that way, but how long do you put your life on hold when you're the one who has to make the change?"

I give her hand a squeeze before letting it go. "I'm so sorry, Chloe."

She shrugs. "It's not like I can do anything about it, so I needed to make a decision for me and my boys." She takes a deep breath, smiles, and swipes another French fry off my plate.

I just laugh and shake my head. Some things never change.

"So, what about you? Are you married? Kids?" she asks between bites.

I blow out a breath. "I was married. No kids. I wanted them, but it turned out she didn't."

Chloe's expression falls. "I'm sorry. My boys drive me crazy, but I wouldn't be without them." She studies me for a moment. "I should have been better at keeping in touch. We were only gone a few months when I fell pregnant, and then we had twins, and our whole focus was on battling through that."

I swallow hard. "I had no idea."

"Scott wouldn't talk about whatever it was you two fell out over, and then my life was taken over by sleepless nights and nappies and the disappointment of having to pull out of university. We put everything into Scott's education, so he could qualify and start making decent money. It wasn't easy, but we got there, and he made sure we were well taken care of if ... when something happened to him." She sucks on her bottom lip. "But I did always wonder what happened to you."

Chloe picks up her drink and takes a sip.

"I married Piper Edwards."

She waves her hand in the air and coughs, her other hand covering her mouth as she tries so hard not to laugh. I reach over to pat her between the shoulder blades, but she shakes her head, tears rolling down her cheeks.

"Sorry. I shouldn't have reacted that way." She sniffs, wiping the tears away. "That was not a name I expected to hear."

I clamp my lips together in bemusement. She's right, but at the time I thought Piper was the right choice. She loved me, and I fell for her. And I wanted it to work right up until I caught Piper in bed with our neighbour.

"Why didn't you expect to hear her name?"

Chloe smiles. "You two weren't exactly friendly in school. Although I did always wonder if she had a crush on you."

"We had a bit of a love hate relationship for a while, but she was there for me when you two left, and I was crazy about her. For a while, anyway. We had mostly good times, some not so good times, and then she had an affair." I look down at my beer. "It broke me."

Her brows knit. "I'm sorry to hear that."

"I didn't think things were quite that bad, you know?" I take a long sip of beer. "What happened? To Scott, I mean."

Chloe bites her top lip. "It was a car accident. The other driver crossed the centre line and hit him head on."

"I wish I'd had a chance to say goodbye."

"So do I." Her composure disappears again for a moment. "I still miss him every day. But now I need to work out how to live for me. I'm still not quite sure how, but it's not healthy to live any other way."

Nodding, I study her closely. The pain of losing him is etched in her expression. I'm not sure how I would cope in her position.

"I'm here. Whatever you need from me, I'm here."

Chloe's smile is warm and makes my heart leap despite the topic. "I appreciate that so much. It'll be weird for a while being in a new house, but I think this is a good move. Good for the boys to have family around, and good for me to hang out with old friends."

I grin. "I like the idea of hanging out."

"Me too. I can't tell you how happy I was to see you tonight. I've spent the past week tossing up whether to even go to the reunion. But I'm glad I decided to, even if I didn't stay."

"I'm glad you did too."

I close my eyes in frustration as the text tone comes from my phone. The last thing I need is an interruption from this.

"That's work. I don't get after hours calls very often, but this is something I have to sort out."

"What do you do?" she asks.

"I work in security. I've got my own company that does monitoring and employs guards for various companies. And I've got a bit of a problem right now with one of my employees."

"Anything I can do?"

She's always been so giving.

"Give me your number."

"Only if you give me yours too."

I smile. "That can be arranged."

After we swap numbers, I walk her out to her car.

"I'd really like to do this again," I say.

Chloe nods. "Me too. Maybe next time, with some warning, I can leave the car behind and we can have a real night out."

I can't stop myself from grinning. "Let's plan for that."

"It's been a long time since I've been out even for one meal and a low alcohol beer." She laughs. "I really enjoyed myself."

"I'm glad you're back, Chloe."

She gets up on her tiptoes and kisses me on the cheek. "Me too. Make sure you call me."

I smile. "You bet I will."

SIX

HUNTER

I'M NOT IMPRESSED about being interrupted. And even less impressed about why.

I pull up to the building Gary's supposed to be patrolling outside tonight. The owner's had a series of break-ins with valuable gear stolen, so for now we've set up night-time patrols to keep the place safe.

Thankfully, there are two guards on this job because that's what the customer paid for. I'm also glad it was the other guard who called me and not the client because I could have dealt with a no-show better than I'm about to deal with this.

Gary's slumped against the wall, and the alcohol stench wafts up from him, causing me to grimace.

"Gary. I'm calling you a taxi and sending you home."

"But you said if I missed a shift I'd be fired." The words are slurred. I can't deal with this right now.

"We'll talk about it later. Right now, you need to go home and sleep this off."

I dial the local taxi company, and sigh. Tonight was amazing, and now I'm going to have to pick up a shift to cover Gary at short notice.

I don't mind the work at all, I'm not impressed at having my evening with Chloe cut short.

After pouring him into the taxi, I start the patrol.

It's going to be a long night.

WITH ABOUT THREE HOURS SLEEP, I could do without the rock concert coming from next door. My new neighbours have been quiet so far, and to be fair they're not really that noisy. But I'm tired, and that bass line is doing nothing to make me feel better.

I tug on the spare pillow and pull it over my other ear.

It doesn't really help.

Now I'm awake, there's no point in trying to get back to sleep. I'd never be any good as a regular shift worker.

Dragging myself out of bed, I throw on a pair of shorts and a singlet. While we're drawing closer to autumn, the weather's still ridiculously hot, and while their music bugs me, I envy the swimming pool next door.

I trudge down to the kitchen to make a coffee. It's better that I don't go into the office today. I'd only be angry and do something I'll regret later.

Flicking the kettle on, I grab my phone from the kitchen bench where I dropped it earlier this morning to text Liz.

Me: *I'm not in the office today. Gary turned up drunk for his shift last night. Will deal with it tomorrow.*

Dropping my phone back down, I spoon two teaspoons of instant coffee in my cup. I'll need an extra caffeine boost to get through today. Later on, I'll head to the gym and work it out, although that'll probably be followed by a burger.

After I've added the hot water, I take my coffee into the living room and place it on the table while I sit on the couch and rub my temples.

Working an unexpected eight-hour shift last night isn't helping my mood whatsoever, and I need to sort out Gary and work on finding someone to replace him.

I should be on cloud nine after seeing Chloe last night.

The memory of her warm smile makes my heart thud. She's every bit as beautiful as I remember, and sweet. There's some deep grief there that I understand. I can't really believe Scott's dead, but her eyes tell a story of the pain she's been through.

Seeing that pain makes me want to be there for her.

And even though we hadn't seen each other for years, there's a hole in my heart where Scott used to be. It's a bitter pill to swallow that he's gone. We were kids when our friendship died, and there was always a part of me that thought maybe one day I'd get my friend back in some capacity.

Now the chance of that happening is gone forever.

The music next door switches up, and I grip my hair. I know they're moving in, and I should be more patient, but I've got used to the peace and quiet around here. Hopefully, this isn't the new normal.

Though, I do need to go and talk to them at some point. There's a gap in the back fence that needs to be repaired. It's been there for a long time, but back when I was married, we left it because we were such good friends with the neighbours and it made it easy for us to go back and forward.

Except maybe it was a little too easy.

But that's a bridge I'll cross at some point. For now, I'm going to drink my coffee, and the paperwork I had planned can also wait for another day.

I pick up my cup, lean back and take a long sip. Maybe I'll go back to bed for a while, and then call Chloe a little later. It's been a long time since I was out anywhere, and last night was good for me, and I think it was good for her.

I jump in my seat and spill coffee all over my chest and lap when glass shatters in my kitchen.

"What the hell?" Shooting to my feet, I peel my wet shirt from my body and slam my now half-empty mug on the table.

I head toward the kitchen, grabbing a fresh shirt from a pile of clean washing as I go. Tugging it on as I survey the damage, I'm just thankful I wasn't standing in there when it happened.

I pick up a large chunk of glass on the bench and shake my head before dropping it back down and stomping out the door.

It takes me no time at all to find the source of my problem.

Two teenage boys stand in the back yard, one holding a cricket bat. I didn't see the ball in the kitchen, but no doubt it's in there.

"What the hell?" I yell.

"Sorry. Oh my God, I'm so sorry."

I can't see them clearly, but I hear the remorse in his voice. It makes no difference right now.

Turning, I walk down the side of the house and out the front. It seems a little presumptuous to walk straight into their back yard, no matter how pissed I am.

Through the gate, I walk up the path to the front door and hammer on it.

"Just a minute." A woman's voice comes from inside the house. She flings open the door. "What's the emergency?"

My mouth falls open.

She's wearing denim cut-offs and a grey shirt that's tight across her breasts. I already think Chloe's beautiful, but she's mouth-watering right now. Her hair's pinned up into a ridiculous small ponytail, and I've never seen her wear glasses before.

She is hot with a capital H and I'm dumbstruck.

"Hunter? Did I tell you where we lived? How did you find me?" She breaks into a breathtaking smile, and for a moment I forget where I am let alone why I'm here.

"Chloe? I didn't know you lived here. Uh ..."

"Mum, I'm so sorry. We were playing cricket and Xander bowled the worst he's ever bowled." A teenage boy appears behind Chloe.

Another, identical boy appears on her other side. "That's debatable. There's nothing wrong with my bowling."

"I hit it, didn't I? And I hit it well." He's so smug, but then he shifts his focus to me and immediately deflates. "And then I broke the window."

"*My* kitchen window," I growl.

Chloe's eyes widen. "Wait. You live next door?"

I nod. "I do."

"And my boys broke your window? Oh my God, I'm so sorry, Hunter. I'll pay for it, and these two will be much more careful. Won't you, boys?"

They both hang their heads and speak in unison. "Yes, Mum."

"Come in for a coffee and we'll sort it out." She smiles and I don't even really care about the window anymore. "Boys, this is Hunter. He was a good friend of your dad's when we were growing up."

The boy on the left lifts his head. "Really? You knew my dad?"

"I did."

His eyes fill with excitement. I guess if he's sixteen and Scott died four years ago, he was only twelve. What are his memories like of his father? Maybe I can fill some gaps for him.

He smiles. "That's so cool."

"Your questions can wait." Chloe crosses her arms. "First, I'm making coffee and maybe we can have some of that chocolate cake I made this morning. And you two can apologise again to Hunter."

"Sorry, Hunter," the boy on the left says.

Chloe turns to the other boy. "Xander?"

"Sorry," he mumbles.

That one. I recognise the pout. They're both like Scott in looks, but one's more like him than the other.

"Come in, Hunter. I'll move these two out of the way so we can get through." She turns and gives both boys a shove down the hallway that leads to the back of the house. "Sorry the place is a bit of a mess. We've still got a lot of unpacking to do, and I've been working today."

"Don't apologise." I follow her through to the kitchen. I know this house well. We were friends with the people who used to live here until my wife decided to fuck the man of the house. "I didn't even know you'd moved in."

"We've only been here a few days."

The woman by the pool. It's like a light bulb goes off over my head, and without thinking, my gaze dips to Chloe's arse to check it out.

Yep. That's her.

One of the boys clears his throat, and I look up and shoot him a sheepish look.

"How do you take your coffee? It's instant at the moment because I have no idea which box the coffee machine is in, but I'm sure I'm not that far off finding it." She opens a cupboard and bends over, retrieving two coffee cups from it.

Holy shit! This isn't fair. None of this is fair.

"Do you want a drink, Braden and Xander?" she asks.

"I'll get some juice out of the fridge. Want one, Xan?" Braden asks.

Xander shakes his head and raises an eyebrow at me. I shrug.

"Um ... milk and two sugars, Chlo. Thanks."

She smiles as she spoons the coffee into the mugs, looking back over her shoulder at me. "No one's called me that for a long time."

I laugh. "You know I picked that up from Scott."

She nods. "Yeah. I used to tease him that he was being lazy because my name was only one more syllable. But I miss it."

"I'll take up the mantel, then." I grin.

"Take a seat at the table and I'll bring this over with the cake. Braden and Xander, sit down and talk to Hunter. I'm sure you can ask him anything about your dad."

I cross the room and sit at the table. Braden smiles as he sits down with his juice while Xander crosses his arms and glares at me.

"So you were Dad's friend?" Braden asks.

"I was his best friend, except for your mother."

"Then why haven't we ever heard of you?" Xander has that suspicious tone that Scott always had. He was the biggest sceptic I ever met and questioned everything. I bet his kids do the same.

I blow out a breath. "Your dad and I had a falling out before he left town to go to uni. It was stupid, and I'll always regret we never patched things up." I pause. "Your mum told me you look a lot like your dad, and you do."

The atmosphere shifts a little as he shuffles in his seat. "You think so?"

"You're what, sixteen? Your dad and I were really close at that age. You two are the spitting image of him at sixteen. I'm sorry I didn't get to see him before he died. But I'm really glad to meet the two of you."

"Here we go." Chloe places the two cups of steaming coffee on the table before turning back to return to the bench. She comes back with a plate of cake and some smaller plates, which she places in front of us all. "Now, about this window."

"I'll call the glass place when I get home and get them to come out."

"Let me know how much it is and I'll pay for it."

My anger over the broken window is completely gone. Not just because it's Chloe, although, that's a huge part, but because these two kids probably would have been playing with their dad if he was still here. Scott loved cricket, and he would have loved playing it with his sons.

"Sure thing." I turn to Xander. "Your dad was a decent bowler. We used to play in my parents' backyard all the time. We might also have broken a window or two back then."

His lips twitch. "We used to play with him back at the old house. He was alright."

I nod. "If you have any questions about him, just ask. I'd be happy to share."

A hand closes over mine, and I look back at Chloe. Gratitude fills her expression. "Thank you."

"You're welcome." I shoot her a smile.

She blushes and looks back down at her coffee as she lifts her hand.

"Would you play cricket with us?" Braden asks.

The question takes me by surprise. I haven't played in years, and my chest tightens at the thought of playing backyard cricket with Scott's sons. There was a time in my life I thought I'd be doing that kind of thing with my own children, but that never worked out.

"Braden, I'm sure Hunter—"

"Sure. I'd love to at some point. But not today because I had to work unexpectedly last night and after I've called the glass place, I'm going to get some sleep."

Chloe focuses her gaze on me. "What happened last night?"

"Just some work stuff. I'll get it sorted when I'm not so cranky."

"You? Cranky?"

In all fairness, she doesn't know how angry at the world I was when Piper and I broke up. How I screwed my way around town before realising it didn't help. How I had a hardened reputation well before that, which led, in part, to my career choice.

"I'm not really the man you used to know, Chlo. Things changed a lot while you were away."

Her smile falters and she studies my expression closer. She's not seen that side of me, the one that protects itself from hurt because I have no barriers when it comes to her. I never did.

"Things changed a lot for me too. I guess we have a lot of years to catch up on." Her soft tone puts me at ease.

"We do." I smile.

"Mum, we're going to go and pick up our cricket gear." Braden and Xander stand.

She nods. "Good idea."

She's silent as she watches them leave before turning back to me.

"And in the meantime, we have some other stuff to sort."

"Like what."

"The window?"

Shit. "Yeah. We can sort that out later. I'll go and call the glass company now."

She smiles. "Thanks, Hunter. I'm glad you're next door. It'll be good to spend time together and catch up properly."

"It will." I swallow hard. I'm like that awkward fifteen-year-old again who just realised how much he liked his best friend's girlfriend. I can't shake her hand, or she'll discover just how sweaty my palms are.

"And thank you for offering to talk to the boys. They like hearing about their dad."

"You're welcome." I hesitate. "I'll text you later?"

"I'll look forward to it."

She stands and rounds the table, sliding her arms around my waist as if it's second nature. I close my eyes because it feels so good.

This takes me back to when we were kids. Chloe was always the one who showed her affection openly. She was often the opposite of Scott, and there were times I wondered how they worked. But they did.

Maybe she's the key to opening me up again.

SEVEN

CHLOE

THERE ARE days when I almost feel like my old self.

And on those days, I'm full of energy and ready to face the world head on with whatever it wants to throw at me. Then there are the bad days. When they come, I don't want to get out of bed in the morning. I want to bury myself under the covers and pretend the world doesn't exist. Those are the days when I barely recognise myself.

A mother at eighteen, I grew up fast, and I never regretted any of it. Now I'm haunted by the past, and sometimes I feel like I'm about a hundred years old. Grief ages you. It tears down any defences you have and hides deep inside just waiting for its moment. And then it hits you right between the eyes and knocks you out.

Thankfully, the bad days are low in number now.

Early on, I felt like a zombie as I went through the mechanics of just getting through the day. I became embedded in the routine of life. Take the boys to school, come home and try to write, pick up the boys from school. It became important to us, and got us all through those moments of overwhelming grief.

There's no routine here just yet.

The boys started school this week, and they have a love hate thing going on with my insistence that I drive them to school. I know I tease them about learning to drive and we talk about buying a car, but I'll never admit to them that the thought of them going out in the world by themselves scares the shit out of me.

There are less cars on the road here than back in Auckland, and the drive to school is peaceful in comparison to what it used to be. I'm thankful for small mercies, but no less scared for them. I know it's human nature to worry about your children, and I fight it consuming me all the time.

I walk out into the sun and raise my face. The weather is definitely a bonus here, and I'm so lucky the house has a swimming pool.

And during the day I have it all to myself.

I love that Hunter's my neighbour. We just clicked the other night like we always did. He was as good a friend to me as he was to Scott, and now all I feel is shame that I didn't reach out to him. I left well enough alone when Scott told me their friendship was irreparable. And then my own life took a twist with my pregnancy, which put everything else on the backburner.

Picking up the leaf scoop, I drag it across the surface of the pool, collecting the few leaves scattered on the surface.

Scott would have loved this, but I can't help but wonder if I made a mistake coming here, and whether this specific house was the right choice.

He wraps his arms around my waist and buries his face in my neck.

"Remember that house I told you I wanted to buy back home? I still look out for it. It's still my dream to buy it for you."

"Scott," I whisper.

"Maybe one day we'll retire there. The kids will be grown up and gone, and we can fool around in the swimming pool."

I laugh. "What is it with you and the swimming pool?"

"I've spent a lot of years imagining us there." He links his fingers

in mine. "And like every dream, there's usually some kind of fantasy that involves you."

"You are terrible, Scott Cooper."

He shakes his head. "No. Just completely and utterly in love with my wife."

I drop to my knees. Memories like that make it hard to breathe, and I clutch at my chest, sobbing.

The grief is overwhelming.

Scott should be here with us. He should be standing by the pool, rake in hand, smiling that devilish smile at me because the boys are in school and it's just us.

So often these days I regret that we never had any more children. He wanted to, once he started earning good money as a lawyer, but the twins were a handful already and we kept putting it off.

And putting it off.

The agony of not giving him what he wanted hits me and I cry harder at the thought. This was supposed to be our home, and all of a sudden I'm second guessing myself because I thought moving here would give me a sense of closure.

In some ways it has, but in other ways it's the one place I'll always struggle with memories.

Strong arms wrap around me, and I'm pulled into a hard chest.

My heart races, and I plant one palm, pushing away.

"Chloe. It's me."

I look up, right into Hunter's dark eyes.

It's overwhelming.

He holds me tight while I weep on his shoulder, before scooping me into his arms and carrying me into the house.

Sitting on the couch, he holds me. It's comforting, and just what I needed in a weird way.

He cradles me on his lap as I rock, pressing a kiss into my hair like a protective parent.

"Thank you."

. . .

"I ... I was standing on the back porch and saw you crying. I couldn't leave you there when you were so upset. Are you okay? What's wrong?"

I swallow hard. "It's stupid. It's been four years."

"Sometimes a lifetime isn't enough when you lose someone you love."

"It was my fault," I whisper.

He doesn't say anything, and I guess he can't. No one knows what happened that day but me.

"It was a Friday night, and the boys were having a sleepover with a friend. Scott got caught up at work. I called him to come home because we had the place to ourselves ..."

Hunter palms my cheek, slots his fingers into my hair and raises my face until his gaze meets mine. "You loved him, and you wanted to be with him. It makes sense."

I bite my lower lip. "If ... if I hadn't called him, he wouldn't have been on the road when she crossed the centre line. I'd still have him here."

Tears roll down my cheeks. I've never told anyone this before, but Hunter's the one person I know will be on my side.

"You weren't to know that, Chloe. There's no way to turn back time. All you can do is live for the future." His brown eyes search mine. "And you have me now. I'm here whenever you need me."

"I'm sorry to do this to you."

Hunter shakes his head. "Anything you need. I'm right next door."

"I can't ask that of you."

He leans his forehead against mine. It's an intimate gesture, but instead of me feeling freaked out, it's comforting. *He's* comforting.

"Our friendship means you can ask anything of me. At any time. And I don't say that to many people." He pulls back. "You are the one exception."

"Why?"

"I care, Chloe. I always did."

I swallow hard, and squeeze him tighter.

"Thank you. That means so much."

Hunter was always there for Scott and me, so it makes sense he would be here for me now too. But his actions tell me there's something more to it. And for once I wish I had more experience with men to know whether I'm right.

"Do the boys need a ride home from school?"

I shake my head. "I'll go and get them. Xander's got his try-out for the school rugby team today, and Braden's going for support, so they'll text when they're ready."

"You're not going anywhere. Not after this. You look exhausted. Are you even sleeping properly?"

I bite my bottom lip to stop myself from laughing. "Yes, Dad."

He frowns. "Don't you ever call me that again."

I wipe the tears that have pooled in my eyes with the back of my hand and then laugh, and it takes away some of the pain. But only for a little while.

"Chloe, I'm serious."

"My sleep has been hit and miss the past four years. I'm used to it."

"Go and have a nap. I'll pick up the boys."

I hesitate. I've never let anyone do that before. It's been one of the things I can control.

"I'm not sure—"

"I've got this. Don't worry about anything."

It's been so long since anyone has said that to me, and all it does is bring up fresh tears.

"Thank you," I whisper.

"Anything for you. I only wish you'd come home earlier for me to take care of you. Because I know you, and I know you were used to someone who always had your back, and I don't think you've had that for some time."

I shake my head. He's right. I always knew I had Caleb, but he was only there for visits. I've done things by myself for so long, and it's not always easy.

"I've never trusted anyone else to drive my boys except Caleb. Not since ..."

He takes my hand in his. "I understand. I'd never let anything happen to them. You can trust me."

I take some deep breaths. "Bring them straight home."

His confident smile gives me strength. "I'll do better than that. I'll bring them home and feed them while you take a rest."

I bite my cheek so hard the coppery taste of blood fills my mouth. But I force myself to nod. I'd call Caleb, but he's sure to be working, and I don't really want to interrupt his day when Hunter's right here making the offer.

"Chloe. I'll keep them safe." He plants a kiss on my forehead and slowly releases his grip on me.

I uncurl and stand in front of him. "I know you will."

"Give me your phone, and when they text I'll go and get them."

I nod and make my way into the kitchen where my phone sits on the bench. Firing off a quick text to Xander to let him know Hunter's picking him up, I take it back to the living room and hand it to Hunter.

He stands, and I can't get over this more grown up version of him. He's undergone a transformation since I've been gone and looks like solid muscle. And then there's the thick beard which suits him. And despite him saying he's changed, I know his heart. It's good, and I know he'll do everything he can to keep my boys safe—to keep Scott's boys safe.

I do trust him.

"Thank you. For everything."

He nods. "We'll be fine. Go and get some rest."

I close my eyes as he wraps his arms around me and gives me a hug.

Maybe I feel a bit helpless when I'm a mess of emotions, but

Hunter centres me.
His friendship means the world.

EIGHT

HUNTER

SEEING Chloe like that rips me apart.

It's clear she's still hurting so much. And I understand it. Those two had a love most people will never find in a lifetime. The loss of that must have been devastating.

It was like second nature to take her in my arms and look after her. I'd do it again in a heartbeat.

She's gone for about an hour when the phone pings. I've been working out what to cook for dinner, but she's filled the pantry, fridge and freezer, so putting together a meal is pretty simple. I'm sure the boys won't care as long as it's food.

Xander: *Hunter's picking us up? Is everything okay? We're ready.*

I smile and pick up Chloe's car keys from the bench. There's no point taking my car when I can use hers. I can't imagine either of those boys will want to climb into the back seat in my coupe.

Locking the house, I walk into the sunshine and to her car in the driveway. I'm glad I decided to work from home for a while. Liz is dealing with Gary and helping him get help, and I'm better off out of it. She's got things running like clockwork anyway, and that suits me.

It's not a long drive to the school, but coming here takes me back every time.

"When I get to Auckland ..."

"You're so selfish," I mutter.

"What?"

"It's all 'I' and 'me'. Chloe's going with you too. Do any of your plans include her?"

He narrows his eyes. "You know they do."

"Doesn't sound like it."

"Dude. What is your problem?" He laughs, but it sounds nervous.

"All your plans centre around you. Chloe has needs too. Are you even thinking about that?"

His brow furrows. "Of all people, you know I am. All the time. What the hell is your ..."

It's like a lightbulb goes off over his head. "You like her."

"She's my best friend's girlfriend. Of course I do."

"No. It's more than that." Scott always knew me so well. I have no idea how he never worked it out before. "Shit. You've got the hots for her."

I don't say anything. I can't deny it. I've been in love with Chloe since the summer of my sixteenth year, when I got dumped by a girl whose name I can't even remember now, and she was there for me.

"Scott—"

Anger flares across his face. "When I say 'I', I mean 'we'. Chloe and I might as well be one person. I'm going to marry her, Hunter, and we're going to have a family and a life far from here. Far from you."

He shakes his head as he walks away. I'm sure he'll calm down.

But he didn't. He guarded that relationship as the most precious thing he ever had, and it was. I'm not sure it was even healthy for him to be so possessive of her. But their relationship was their business, and I didn't pursue it after they left.

I wish I had. I wish I'd had the chance to talk things out with him before he died. We were just kids when it happened with no real idea about what the future would bring.

And now all these years later, Chloe's the one back in my life. Along with the two boys walking toward the car who look so much like their father. At least I can tell them apart, as Xander's in his rugby gear.

"Hey. What's going on?" Xander asks.

"Your mum wasn't feeling well, so I'm picking you up and then cooking dinner."

His eyebrows rise. "Is she okay?"

"She'll be fine. She just needs some rest."

I pop the boot so they can put their bags away, and Xander glares at Braden until he steps back and lets him in the front seat.

"So, what's wrong with Mum?" Xander asks.

With them buckled in, I start the car. "She got a bit upset today thinking about your dad."

He frowns. "That hasn't happened for a while."

"How bad was it?" I ask.

He hesitates.

"Really bad." Braden speaks from the back seat. "She cried all the time and tried to hide it from us. But we could see it."

"She stopped eating." Xander's voice makes me turn my head toward him. "Grandma still gives her shit about how thin she is."

"Our other grandma doesn't really like Mum anymore," Braden says.

"What? She loved Chloe when we were growing up."

"Not anymore. She tries to bully Mum, but Mum's really good at telling her to back off." Xander's voice has a tinge of pride when he says it.

I don't know how to process this. It's been a long time since we were all kids hanging out at each other's homes, and I spent a lot of time at both Scott's place and Chloe's with my parents split. Both sets of parents were equally caring, and as Chloe's parents adored Scott, Scott's parents adored Chloe.

What the hell happened?

Slipping the car into gear, I indicate and pull out.

"You're the first person other than Uncle Caleb to pick us up from school. Mum must trust you," Braden says.

I nod. "I had to talk her into it, but we're good."

"Why do you have her car?"

I chuckle. These two are a lot like their father, always full of questions. It's what would have made Scott a good lawyer.

"She doesn't know I have it. I figured you'd prefer to be able to get in easy rather than one of you squeeze into the backseat of mine. Neither of you are exactly short."

Braden snorts with laughter.

We ride the rest of the way in silence, but it's not uncomfortable. Both boys have opened up their world to me, and I can't take that for granted. It'll be essential for any ongoing relationship with Chloe.

And if she can lean on me when she needs to, I'm only too happy to do it.

I'll be the rock she needs.

XANDER LOOKS around the room as we step into the kitchen.

The vegetables are all set out ready for me to cut up and cook, and the meat's defrosting in a bowl of water.

"We can cook dinner," he says.

"I told your mother I would. Besides, I'm glad we get to spend some time together. I'll answer your questions about your dad, and you can tell me all about your lives."

Braden shrugs. "There's not much to tell."

"Really?" I smile at the sight of Xander picking up the potato peeler. "Didn't you go and live in the UK for a while?"

Braden nods. "Yeah, when we were little. And then we came back when we were about ten."

"That'll be why you don't have much of an English accent."

"Braden had one way stronger than me," Xander says. "Dad used to say it made it easier to tell us apart."

I laugh. "Today, it was easy. I'm not sure about any other day of the week."

"You'll get used to us." Braden laughs.

The boys go into the living room once everything's cooking, and turn on the television. I switch between the two rooms, keeping an eye on dinner, while slowly making progress with them. Braden's more open than Xander, but both of them ask me questions and I answer as best I can.

I reach the point of the meal where I start cooking the steak, and they both walk in as the scent fills the room.

"I hope you two like steak. She said you ate just about anything, and I noticed there was a lot in the freezer." The pan sizzles as I flip over the meat.

"Yeah. Smells amazing." Braden approaches. "Dad never cooked for us. Mum said he was terrible."

I chuckle. "Yeah, he was never very good. We did home economics lessons like everyone else, and Scott was smart at everything else except for cooking."

Braden grins. "We used to beg Mum to have a night out because we knew Dad would buy takeaways."

"That sounds like Scott. Let me guess ... Pepperoni pizza?"

Even Xander cracks a smile. "That was his favourite."

"And no pineapple under any circumstances." Braden laughs.

"I agree with him there." I shake the other pan full of crispy potatoes. "You guys hungry?"

"Starving," Braden says.

"Well, wash up and take a seat, and I'll serve this up."

The two of them disappear out of the kitchen, and I breathe a sigh of relief. I meant what I said to Chloe about being there for her whenever she needs me, but I wasn't sure how the boys would receive this. It's one thing to be sharing a coffee with their mother. It's quite another to take over the kitchen and cook dinner. But they seem to have taken it in their stride.

Being accepted by them is really important to me.

I open a couple of cupboards before finding the dinner plates, and pull four out. Spreading them on the kitchen bench, I place a generous helping of steamed mixed vegetables, crispy potatoes, and a lovely piece of scotch fillet on each.

It's not as good reheated, but I want to make sure there's a meal for Chloe when she does wake up.

The boys reappear, and I nod toward the table. "I'll serve this up in a second."

With Chloe's plate stored in the fridge, I place a meal in front of each boy before sitting at the table with them.

"This looks so good," Braden says.

"I don't think I'm too bad a cook. I've had years of practice."

The two of them start eating, and you'd think they hadn't eaten for years.

"You two remind me a lot of your dad. He ate like that too." I chuckle.

Braden grins. "Mum says we have hollow legs."

"When we were kids, we'd go and get a big feed of fish and chips. Chloe would eat like a sparrow, and maybe have half a piece of fish and a handful of chips. Scott would make sure she'd had enough and then demolish the rest of it. I have no idea where he put it."

Braden laughs before taking another bite, and Xander eyes me warily. He's still eating, so at least he trusts me enough for that.

"How long did you know my dad?" Xander asks.

I draw in a deep breath. "We started school around the same time. So, when we were five. I was there when he met your mother. That was a few years later."

He's quiet for a moment. "You didn't stay friends with him."

I swallow down the hurt that hits me. While I was sure they'd have questions about how we could be such good friends and yet never see each other, this is hard.

"We had a falling out before he went to university. It was just some stupid teenage thing that got blown out of all proportion." I take in a deep breath. "I'll always regret we didn't patch things up before he died. But he and your mum moved away and never came back."

"That sucks," Braden says.

I nod. "It does." I take another bite and look at Xander. "Hey, how did your rugby go today?"

He shrugs. "I don't know yet. I think it went alright."

I shift my gaze to Braden. "What about you? Do you play sport other than backyard cricket?"

Braden screws up his face. "I play in the backyard, but I hate sport otherwise."

"Braden's the geek of the family," Xander says.

I shrug. "Everybody's different."

We eat the rest of the meal in silence before Braden looks up. "Is there more?"

Grinning, I nod toward the cooktop. "The meat's all gone, but there are plenty of potatoes and vegetables."

"The potatoes are great. Thanks, Hunter."

I turn to Xander. "How about you? Want some more?"

I'm rewarded with a nod. If I hadn't known their father so well, I might be more concerned, but Xander touches my heart in a way I didn't anticipate because he is so much like Scott. It makes me miss his father more but makes me grateful that I can at least get to know his sons.

Both boys get up and grab a second helping.

"We'll do the dishes, right, Xan?" Braden says.

Xander nods. "It's just loading the dishwasher."

"Still, I'm sure your mum will appreciate it." I smile at them both before shovelling food into my mouth.

"What's happening here?"

Chloe's smile is tired, but her eyes are full of affection as she takes in the sight of the three of us.

"Hunter cooked dinner, and now we're doing the dishes. Go back to bed, Mum," Braden says.

She meets my gaze.

"There's a plate for you in the fridge, Chlo. I'll heat it up for you. It's probably a good idea for you to have something to eat."

Her smile grows. "I can heat it up. Thank you, Hunter."

She crosses the room and opens the fridge.

I finish up my meal and Braden grabs my plate to put into the dishwasher. He and Xander work together, loading it up as the microwave beeps and Chloe makes her way to the table.

"This looks good," she says.

"The boys seemed to like it. I'll come around and cook whenever you need me to."

She smiles, and cuts a piece of steak off, letting out a moan as she slides it into her mouth. I'm probably going to have a heart attack right here watching her eat.

"That's so good. I might have to keep you on."

I smile. "Glad you like it."

"Considering I've cooked dinner I don't know how many nights out of the last seventeen years, it's nice to have a break. Most nights, anyway."

She scoops some potato into her mouth and lets out another moan, and it sounds so hot, I'm going to have to leave at this rate before I embarrass myself.

I shift in my seat. "So, I was wondering if you wanted to go out for dinner at Darren and Meredith's."

"Carmichael?" she asks, as she slices another piece of steak.

I nod. "Meredith has been asking me over for dinner for ages, but I haven't been. This time she asked about you after our disappearance from the reunion. Dinner's on Saturday."

Chloe gazes at me. "I need to get her number from you so I can call her."

"I thought you might come with me. We can always leave if you get uncomfortable."

She nods. "I'd like that."

"Trust me. I'll have you out of there in a heartbeat if it's too much."

She touches my arm, and my heart thuds. This woman has an effect on me like no other—even after all this time.

Being in her presence softens my hardness and makes me want to be better.

"I trust you. Let me know when."

"We're done, Mum. There's just your plate to go," Braden says.

"Thanks, you two." She winks at him and then at Xander.

"Thanks for dinner, Hunter," Xander mumbles.

"You're welcome."

It takes a moment for them to leave the room, and I take a deep breath. "I should get going and let you finish and get back to bed."

"Thank you for everything. Today was a tough one," Chloe says.

I reach over and grasp her arm. "Anything you need, I'm right next door."

"I appreciate that."

Leaning forward, I peck her on the cheek. "Have a good rest. I'll let you know about this dinner."

She gives me a tired smile. I'm glad I could be here for her today. I hate the thought of how many days she's been through alone. It must be that much harder to fight your way through the grief of losing a loved one when you're by yourself.

But Chloe isn't alone anymore.

She has me.

NINE

CHLOE

I GLANCE AT HUNTER.

It should feel weird being out with someone who isn't my husband, but he makes me comfortable.

Maybe it's because he came to my rescue when I broke down, or maybe it's because he's the first person I've ever confided in about what happened that day. And he just handled it. He didn't tell me I was a bad person, or that I played a part in what happened.

I'm so glad Hunter's my friend.

As we pull up to Meredith and Darren's house, I almost have to duck my head to see the roof through the car window. At two storeys high, they're clearly doing well for themselves.

"Ready?" Hunter asks.

I nod. "As I'll ever be."

He grins. "That's my girl. Come on."

I follow him up the driveway and to the front door. He knocks, and when Darren opens the door, he looks past Hunter and directly at me.

"Chloe. It's so good of you to come. You had us worried the other night."

I smile. "I'm fine. Thank you for worrying."

He steps out to kiss me on the cheek.

"Uh, you know I'm here too, right?" Hunter laughs.

"You I can see any time." Darren grins and shakes Hunter's extended hand. "Come in. Meredith made a bit of a dinner party of it. I hope you're ready."

I exchange a glance with Hunter. From his expression, this wasn't what he expected either, but I follow him and Darren into the house.

"Chloe." Meredith greets me. She's in the living room with other people I don't recognise. I draw in a deep breath. I'll be okay—I attended enough dinners in my life with legal people I barely knew, but it's still a little awkward. "I'm so glad you're here. Come and meet my friends. Chloe, this is my friend Sarah, and Russell works with Darren."

I nod toward them.

"Sarah's been looking forward to you coming to dinner, Hunter." Her eyes flash with mischief, and I swallow down how uncomfortable that makes me. I'm not even sure why; Hunter's not my date.

"Stop it." Sarah blushes and meets my gaze briefly. I turn my head to see Hunter's in conversation with Darren, and has either missed this whole exchange or doing a really good job of pretending he did.

"Chloe's husband was best friends with Hunter when we were at school. I'm sure she has plenty of info on Hunter if you're still interested." Meredith smiles.

She turns to me and grasps my arm. "I was sorry to hear about Scott. And even more sorry that I upset you the other night."

I swallow hard. "It's fine. I should be used to it by now."

"Darren dug up Scott's obituary online. I wish we'd known. We would have made the trip."

"Thanks, Meredith." I'm shaking a little, but I clench and relax my hands a few times to even out.

"But I'm happy you're home again. Maybe we can hang out."

I nod. "I'd like that."

She lets me go. "And now I have to go and check on dinner. If you'll excuse me."

I exhale slowly.

"Chloe. Would you like a drink? I have beer and a few different spirits." Darren walks toward me.

"A beer would be great, thanks. I'm not driving." I grin.

He laughs. "Sounds good. I'll get you one. Hunter?"

"Just a juice if you've got one. I am driving." Hunter shoots me a pointed look, and all I can do is laugh.

"Sorry. I could drink a juice in solidarity."

"Have a beer. Enjoy yourself." He chuckles.

Darren's gaze flickers between us. He seems to be biting down a smile. "Beer and a juice coming right up."

I take a deep breath as he leaves the room, and we're left with Sarah and Russell.

"It's good to meet you two," Hunter says.

Sarah moves closer. "We've met before."

"Have we? I'm sorry if I can't remember."

Her expression darkens before she breaks into a brilliant smile. "I'll just have to remind you."

I drop my gaze. It's really obvious what she wants, and it makes me a little uncomfortable. I mean, Hunter can hook up with whomever he likes, but I don't want to see it.

"Here we go." Darren heads straight to me and hands me a Corona bottle before giving Hunter his juice. "How are you settling back into town, Chloe? Good?"

"It has been. The house is perfect, and we're mostly unpacked."

"Is it good to be home?"

I glance at Hunter. "It's really good. I think it's been the right thing for us to do." I take a sip of my beer. "Our old house was getting to be a bit much. We're going to form some new memories here."

"Dinner's nearly done, so maybe we should take a seat." Meredith smiles as she walks into the room, guiding us toward the dinner table.

"Hunter, you're here between me and Sarah. Chloe, you're on the other side next to Russell," Meredith says. "I'll just serve dinner."

I exchange a glance with Hunter and smile. His tight-lipped expression shows he's not as okay with this as me. But this isn't a date, and even though he's already become my rock, I need to stand on my own two feet.

He's still right across the table from me.

Sarah's pretty glamorous in comparison to me. I'm not even wearing makeup, just a bit of lip gloss, but she looks like she walked out of a magazine.

I don't even know why I'm thinking that. It's not a competition.

She flashes me a smile before she takes a seat beside Hunter.

My cheeks burn, and I dip my head to avoid eye-contact.

"Are you okay, Chloe?" Darren asks.

I look up. "I'm fine. I don't get out of the house often, so this is nice."

He smiles at me. Apart from Hunter, Scott didn't have a lot of close friends other than me. And I was a bit of a loner other than Scott. It's wonderful to be welcomed into Darren and Meredith's home when we weren't close previously.

"You're welcome any time."

I watch as he disappears into the kitchen behind his wife.

"Chlo."

I shift my gaze to Hunter.

"Are you okay?"

"I'm fine. What is it with you guys asking me?"

He shrugs. "Just checking."

"I appreciate it, but I'm okay."

His gaze stays on me, and I brush my hands down my skirt, smoothing the fabric and taking a deep breath.

"How's business, Hunter? You work in security, don't you?" Sarah asks.

He turns his head and nods. "Business is good."

She smiles, and then her unimpressed gaze hits me. I smile

sweetly back, pick up my handbag where I've dropped it on the floor beside me, and pull out my coconut lip gloss. It's a nervous habit to apply it more often, and I'm aware of it, but I figure it's pretty harmless.

I pop the lid, place my index finger in the container and scrape some over my lips. The familiar scent helps calm me, but when I look up and see Hunter's gaze focussed on my mouth, the effects are reversed. I smack my lips together and throw the gloss back in my bag.

"Here we go." Meredith says, and she and Darren place plates in front of us containing pasta with a creamy chicken sauce.

"Looks great. Thank you." I smile at Meredith.

I wait until she and Darren join us with their own plates before picking up my knife and fork.

"It's Darren's favourite. Hope you like it."

"I'm sure I will."

She smiles at me, and I cut a slice of chicken. It's full of flavour and I nod, moaning at the taste. "That's so good."

"I'll give you the recipe if you'd like."

"My boys would love this."

"Chloe's boys even eat my cooking. They'll love the crap out of his."

I laugh at Hunter's comments. "To be fair, you're a good cook too."

Meredith looks between us. "You two have been having dinners together?"

"Hunter helped me out the other day." I scoop another piece of chicken and pasta into my mouth. It really is delicious. "I wasn't feeling well, so he fed my boys while I had a nap."

"Are you okay now?"

I nod. "The whole move has just been exhausting. Physically and mentally."

"I'm sure."

We continue to eat in silence for a little while before Sarah sparks up a low conversation with Hunter. He glances at me before turning toward her. I know he's feeling a little protective after the other day, and I appreciate it. But she really is pretty, and the two of them would look good together.

That thought doesn't help my unease.

"So, what do you do?" Russell asks.

I turn toward him. "I'm a writer."

He smiles. "Really? Would I know any of your books?"

"I write mystery thrillers under the name C Cooper."

Meredith touches my hand. "I couldn't help overhearing. Those are *your* books?"

I sit up straight. "They sure are."

"I love them. I think I've got all of them." She smiles.

"Really? Don't tell me what you think." I laugh.

"They're so good. The twists always get me. Where does all that come from?"

I shrug. "The real world is a pretty twisted place."

Meredith cocks her head. "That's true. And dark."

"Some years are darker than others." My writing changed a lot after Scott died. I found myself delving deeper to create stories that sold better than anything I'd written before. It took a couple of years for that darkness to lift, and by then I could almost write what I wanted and it would sell.

No one knew who I was, and I didn't hide it, but I also didn't do book tours. No one cared as long as my books sold, and I got privacy with my kids.

"Yes, some years *are* darker than others."

Across the table, Sarah flicks her dark hair, and leans in.

I've seen this before. It conjures up memories of the first dinner Scott and I had with the partners of the law firm he worked for in the UK. His co-worker had sat across the table and flirted with him, but Scott had smiled and stayed focussed on me, his *wife*.

Hunter doesn't do the same. Of course he doesn't. His attention's on Sarah as she talks to him, his long fingers stroking his thick beard.

The rumble of his deep voice resonates, but I can't hear what he's saying with their conversation so quiet.

"So, you're good with words." Russell's voice knocks me out of my stupor.

I shrug. "I guess. When the mood strikes."

I'm not sure what it is about him, but I'm not at ease with this guy.

I freeze when Russell's warm hand lands on my knee. "I'd love to hear more. Maybe I could interest you in going for a drink sometime."

Brushing my skirt down, I push his hand away. "I'm sorry, but I don't think so."

I'm not interested. This guy is making my skin crawl.

"How do I change your mind?"

His hand is back, and I suck in a breath. I learned a long time ago that while most men aren't dickheads, there are definitely those who decide, because you're alone, that it means you'll sleep with anyone.

The assumption seems to double when you're a single mother.

"Look, Russell. I'm sure you're very nice, but I'm not interested."

I shove his hand away more forcibly this time. It's under the table, and I don't want to draw unnecessary attention to it, but that doesn't mean he has any right to put his hands on me.

I feel Hunter's presence before I even notice he's on his feet.

"Get up." Hunter looks past me and at Russell.

"What?" Russell laughs.

"Get up and away from Chloe. Do you think I don't know what you've been doing?"

I look up at Hunter. "It's okay. I took care of it."

"There should have been nothing to take care of. We're swapping seats."

My cheeks burn as Russell holds up his palms. "Chloe and I were just talking."

"You don't need your hand on her knee to talk to her. How many times did she have to move it?"

All I can do is stare at Hunter. Across the table, and with all the chatter, he can't have had a clear view of what happened, but he must have been paying attention.

And then he reaches down and squeezes my shoulder.

My heart goes into overdrive, fluttering like a butterfly. I can barely focus on what happens next as Russell rises and Hunter takes his place.

What the hell just happened?

And it's not just my heart. It's as if a light bulb went off above my head as I stare at Hunter. He's swapping plates across the table and seems oblivious to me watching as my whole body tingles.

What would it be like to be with Hunter?

I always had a soft spot for him, but never saw him as anything other than a friend. Seeing him again after so long is, in a way, like coming home. He's matured, and become even more handsome than I remember, but he just has that familiarity about him which has made it easy to slip into that friendship.

But now I'm seeing him in a different light.

"Are you okay, Chloe?"

I swallow hard and look over to see him smiling at me. "I'm fine. Thank you."

He shoots me a grin, picks up his knife and fork in those large hands of his, and begins to eat his dinner again.

I can barely focus while looking at those hands. What would it be like to have them on me? I'm not sure I'm going to be able to finish dinner.

I spent the first half of the meal focussing on fending off Russell. But Hunter is a whole other distraction. He's eating and taking part in the dinner conversation, but all I can think about is what he did.

And being with him.

He forks a piece of chicken into his mouth, and I'm captivated by how his jaw works beneath his beard. It looks so soft that I squeeze my knife and fork tight to refrain from reaching out and touching it.

I turn back to my meal, but not without glancing at Sarah. The irritation in her eyes makes my stomach flip.

"Chloe, you said earlier you have children?" Meredith asks.

I turn my head, just blinking for a moment as her words sink in. *Speak, Chloe.*

"Uhh. Yes, I do. Twin boys."

She smiles. "Are they like you or Scott?"

"So much like Scott in looks. If you compare them to Scott as a teenager, you can so see the resemblance. But Braden is more like me in personality, where Xander is very Scott."

"Have you got photos?"

"Sure." I reach down into my bag and pull out my phone. Finding the most recent one, I hand it over to Meredith. "Braden on the left, Xander on the right."

Her eyes widen. "Oh my goodness. They're so big. How old are they?"

"Recently turned sixteen. And both much taller than I am."

"Both pretty good at cricket too. I discovered Chloe was living next to me when they broke my kitchen window," Hunter says.

Meredith's mouth falls open. "No. That's so funny."

"Wasn't at the time, but then I realised who it was. But they're really good kids."

I bite my lip and find his brown eyes glistening as the corners of his mouth tug upward. His jaw twitches, and I struggle to look away from the chiselled contours of his face.

"That's wonderful." Meredith hands me back my phone.

I blink and focus on the screen. "Thank you."

"And you've always got that bit of Scott with you," she adds.

Clenching my phone, my chest tightens. "Every day."

Smiling to myself as I drop my phone back into my bag, I'm so proud of my boys. And even though it's rare for me to have a night out, I miss them.

"You should bring them with you next time. They're older than our kids, but I'm sure it'll be good for them to meet more people."

I nod. "That would be great. Braden will probably love that. Xander tends to keep to himself."

She tilts her head. "Not unlike his dad."

"They look identical, but they're not hard to tell apart," Hunter says.

I laugh. "I still get caught out sometimes, but generally it's pretty easy."

My heart swells thinking of my boys, and even though they'll be in their rooms back home, missing them hits me right in the chest.

They drive me nuts at times, but being apart from them has always been hard.

AFTER DINNER and Meredith's Pavlova for dessert, we all sit in the living room once again. I'm on one end of the couch, Hunter in the middle, with Sarah on his other side.

She's still flirting with him, but I'm trying not to pay attention.

"Chloe."

I turn toward Hunter.

"Want to head home? I'm sure you want to check on the boys."

I clasp my hands. "That would be great."

He stands and I follow suit.

"Going so soon?" Meredith asks.

"I have some work to do, and I'm sure Chloe wants to get home to her kids."

Meredith places her hand on my arm. "We should catch up."

"I'd like that. Want my number?"

"I already got it from Hunter. I'll give you a call, and we'll go out for coffee."

"Sounds good."

"See you later, Chloe." Darren doesn't hold back. His arms are around me before I know it, and he kisses my temple.

"Thanks for everything." I say.

"Any time. We'd love to meet your boys."

My heart warms at the thought. "We'll definitely have to arrange that."

Saying our final goodbyes, we make our way to Hunter's car. He opens the door for me, and my heart flutters all over again.

"I don't know about you, but I really didn't want to stick around any longer. I can't believe that guy had the nerve to put his hands on you." There's still edginess to his voice.

"He was a creep." I shudder. "Thank you."

He fixes his dark-eyed gaze on me. "What for?"

"For what you did. It was ... pretty cool."

He grins. "I'm a pretty cool guy."

That smile. I recognised Hunter the instant I saw him at the reunion despite all the changes in him. His face is more weathered behind the beard, and I think he hides a lot behind it. But that smile always did light up a room.

And now it's lighting up my heart.

I'm crushing on Hunter Emerson and I like it.

He starts the car, and we pull out into the street.

I don't want this part of the night to end.

Looking out of the window, we pass house after house, each building a blurry reel of bricks and picket fences.

"You okay?" Hunter asks.

I turn to look at him. "I enjoyed myself for most of the evening."

He sighs loudly. "I'm sorry I couldn't protect you from that."

"I'm a big girl, Hunter."

He glances at me. "I know, but I feel responsible for you. Scott would have killed me if I ever let anything happen to you."

My cheeks burn. Maybe he's not interested. Maybe this is all just out of some sense of duty to his boyhood friend.

I turn my head away again and go back to looking out the window.

"Scott always was a lucky bastard." He laughs as I swing my gaze back to him. "What? Russell's a jerk who needs to keep his hands to himself. But you have always been gorgeous, Chloe. Inside and out."

I swallow hard.

He takes a deep breath like he's about to say something else, but then he doesn't and I can't stop looking at him.

His focus is on the road, so I take the chance to drink in the sight of him. His lips look so soft.

What would it be like to kiss him?

Part of me feels as if I'm not being faithful to my husband. But I don't want to be alone forever, and being with someone else isn't infidelity.

Hunter thinks I'm gorgeous.

I never thought I was anything special with my honey blonde hair, and freckles all over my nose. But he just made my heart swell with his confession.

I'm more alive than I have been in a very long time, and it's so good.

"Nearly there." He shoots another glance at me, and I smile. "Are you sure you're okay, Chloe?"

My brows twitch. "I'm fine."

He takes the last turn and pulls into our street. Parking the car in his driveway, he's out and around before I even put my hand on the door handle.

"I'll walk you home."

My heart's heavy as we reach my front door.

Despite the rocky start, I don't want the night to end. But how do I spend more time with Hunter while trying to work out these new feelings?

He grasps my arm as I slide the key in the door.

"I'm sorry about that tonight. I thought Meredith would sit us together. And I've heard before how handsy Russell is."

I shrug. "There's nothing for you to be sorry about. What you did was pretty amazing."

His smile breaks through his intensity. "You mean a lot to me, Chlo. I'll always be there for you."

I swallow hard to stop the tears that prick my eyes. Scott was always fiercely defensive of me, and it drove me nuts at times, but I appreciated it. I need to stop comparing the two men, but Hunter's actions tonight were familiar, and they made me feel safe.

He makes me feel safe.

His eyes search mine. "Hey. Are you okay?"

I fling my arms around his waist and bury my face in his chest. I don't have the words to tell him how much he means to me right now, and I never thought coming home would have the added benefit of Hunter.

"I'm just glad you were there with me."

He chuckles, stroking my hair and kissing the top of my head. "Anytime you need me, I'm right here."

For a few moments, we just stand there, and I draw strength from his arms around me. God, how I've missed being held. And Hunter is the best hugger ever with his big, strong frame.

I need to let go before I start having inappropriate thoughts about him.

Again.

I disentangle myself from him and gaze at him. He's such an enigma to me at times, with that bearded face that hides the way he feels. But I know his heart, and it's good, and he genuinely cares for me.

Could it turn into something more?

My stomach flips as he casts his gaze over my face and a wry smile crosses his lips.

Hunter Emerson's stealing my heart.

And for the first time in a long time, I think I might be ready for it.

TEN
CHLOE

WHAT DOES FALLING in love feel like?

For as long as I can remember, it was always Scott and Chloe. Chloe and Scott.

Scott was the boy who shared his chocolate biscuits in his lunchbox with me. He was the boy who held my hand on the way to class. He grew into the man I loved and married, and the man I shared two beautiful children with.

We just always were.

Neither of us ever planned to be without the other. We were joined at the hip from the start and that didn't stop until the day he died.

There was no plan for this.

Hunter's been such a good friend since I returned. There were hints that he was interested, but I ignored them not knowing what was real and what wasn't. I've never been in this position before because I always knew where I stood with Scott.

Last night changed everything.

His intensity over the situation showed me a side of him I'd never seen. He was protective, attentive, and for the first time in my life, I imagined being with someone else.

It's the weirdest feeling, and it leaves me giddy with excitement.

There'll always be a part of me that longs for Scott. I wish with all my heart that he would just walk back in the door and everything would go back to the way it was. But that life disappeared the night the police showed up at my door.

No matter how much I want it, I'll never have that life again.

In two more years, my sons will be starting their adult lives, whether that means university or working, and it'll just be me.

I deserve a life of my own.

And maybe Hunter could be that life.

But would he really want to be? Being with me means more than loving me. It means taking on the fact that I lost the man I thought of as the love of my life, and the father of my two children. And it means taking on my children. We're a package deal.

That's a lot for a man to deal with.

I always thought there'd only be room in my heart for that romantic love with Scott, and it's hard to see past that, but now I can see how Hunter could fit in there too. And it feels right that it's him.

He knew me so well when we were children.

Right now, I need to push that aside because I have to do the one thing I've been putting off since we got here. The boys should see their other grandparents, and at some point I'm going to have to talk to Scott's mother.

It's never fun.

My stomach's in knots as I dial her number.

"Hello."

"Hi, Kay. It's Chloe."

There's a pause. "Chloe. Nice of you to call. Are you settled in?"

So far, so good. But it's always a case of waiting for the hammer to fall.

"We are. So, I thought it would be a good time for us to come and see you. Or you could come to dinner here, whichever works for you?"

I already know what the answer will be. Before, it was easy because it was her visiting us. Now, she's going to want to see us on her terms and in her territory.

"I think it would be best if you come here. I'll cook dinner. I'm sure the boys would love a good home cooked meal."

My teeth grind together. "I'm sure. It'll be a break from the cooking they get from me every night."

"How about tonight?"

It's Sunday, so we can excuse ourselves with the boys having school tomorrow. I'd rather not go at all, but she's given me an out at least.

"Sounds great. I'll let Braden and Xander know. They'll be happy to see you."

"Well, it has been so long. They'll be much happier now they can see their grandparents more often instead of being kept away."

My blood boils. We went where Scott got jobs, but somehow she always makes it about her.

I take a deep breath. "I'm sure. What time would you like us to be there?"

"Make it five-thirty, and we'll have dinner around six. Nice and early. We don't want to keep the boys up too late."

I bite my bottom lip. I'm not sure Braden and Xander will appreciate being treated like little kids, but we'll just go and get it over with and come home.

"Okay. Thanks, Kay."

As I disconnect the call, I breathe a sigh of relief. But there's a good chance she'll save her questions for when we go and I get interrogated about my personal life because I think she wants me to be the grieving widow for the rest of my life. And while I'll always grieve her son, that's not what I want for me.

I want more.

I think I want Hunter.

"BOYS. CAN YOU COME HERE, PLEASE?"

First Braden and then Xander make their way down the stairs and into the living room.

"What's up, Mum?" Xander says.

"We're going to your grandmother's for dinner."

"But her cooking ..." Braden starts.

"Your other grandmother."

His eyes widen. "The one who doesn't like you?"

I bite my cheek. When they were younger, they never picked up on any bad vibes between my mother-in-law and me. But it wasn't long before they both separately noticed the underlying tension.

I've never said a bad word against Kay to them, but they know. This is the first time either of them has voiced it.

"It's not that she doesn't like me."

He snorts. "This is how tonight will go. We'll eat dinner. She'll ask you if you're seeing someone because anyone but Dad is cheating, and then she'll pick on some habit of mine. Or Xander's. And she'll blame you for it."

I place my hand on his arm. "Oh, honey. She loved your dad so much." What else do I say? She loves my boys and I don't want this resentment between them.

"Then she should respect you because he loved you."

I tighten my grip. "I love you, Braden. And I agree with you. But she's handling her grief in her own way, and she loves you and Xander more than anything."

He frowns, but it goes unsaid that we'll go and get this over with.

"We don't have to stay long. She knows you have school in the morning."

"When are we going?" Xander asks.

"Grab anything you want to take and we'll get going now. The last thing we need is to be late."

He rolls his eyes. "I've got my phone. That's all I need."

"Me too," Braden says.

I take a deep breath. "Well, then, let's go."

THE STUFFY CAR makes it so hard to breathe, and I wind the window down a little to get some fresh air flowing and try and ease my anxiety over this visit.

This is the house Scott grew up in. I lost my virginity in this house one weekend while his parents were away. The memory makes me smile—neither of us had any idea what we were doing, but we worked it out.

"Here we are."

"Do we really have to do this?" Xander asks.

"It's just for one evening." I sigh. "Look, guys. She's your grandmother and she loves you. I'm fine."

"I just hate the way she treats you."

I hate the way they've worked this out without me saying anything negative. I hate that my relationship with Kay has reached this point. But I guess it's all the boys have ever known.

We get out of the car and make our way to the door. Kay opens it, her face lighting up at the sight of Braden and Xander. I stand back to let her say hello.

"Chloe."

I nod. "Kay."

"Come in."

We kick off our shoes and step into her home where Preston, Scott's father, is standing with his arms open wide. "Chloe." He embraces me, and I hug him back before stepping aside so he can welcome his grandsons.

Kay kisses me on the cheek. "It's good to see you all."

They lead us into the living room, where we all sit on the couch.

"How's the new house, Chloe?" Preston asks.

I run my fingers through my hair. "It's great. We're settling in. It's a lovely house."

"And how's school?" He turns to the boys.

Xander shrugs.

"Good," Braden says.

"I'll just check on dinner," Kay says.

"Is there anything I can do to help?" I go to stand.

She shakes her head. "No. Everything's under control."

Turning, she disappears into the kitchen.

I hate this. When I was a kid, I'd stand in that kitchen peeling potatoes and helping as best I could. This was my second home. But that all changed so quickly when I fell pregnant. Seventeen years is a long time to hold a grudge.

"Xander tried out for rugby at school," I say to Preston.

He smiles. "Following in your father's footsteps."

Xander nods. "I was too late to finish the cricket season, but I want to play next year if I can."

"What about you, Braden?" He turns to my other side.

"I don't like sport much. But I play on the computer a lot."

I smile to myself.

"Oh, I see those Esports on TV. Some of those young guys make a lot of money."

"Don't encourage him." I laugh.

Braden nudges my arm.

They make small talk with their grandfather while I watch Kay taking plates to the table. This really sucks. But I've tried so many times reaching out over the years.

"Dinner's ready." She appears in the doorway.

"Let's wash our hands and go and eat," I say to the boys.

We all stand and file up the hallway, and I'm just grateful for the small reprieve before heading back to the dining room where we all take our seats.

"Smells amazing," I say to Kay.

She smiles. "I remembered how much the boys loved roast chicken last time we were at your place."

She's gone above and beyond. There's a ton of chicken, a mountain of roast potatoes, and my mouth is watering.

Kay's always been a good cook.

"Help yourselves." She nods toward the boys.

I sit quietly as Braden and Xander pile their plates up, and then the rest of us help ourselves.

At first, everyone's busy eating and I start to relax.

"So, Chloe do you have anyone new in your life?" Kay studies me like I'm under a microscope.

"I'm assuming you're asking me if I'm seeing anyone, and the answer is no." I don't drop my gaze. Not that it's really any of her business, and even if I were, I wouldn't be telling her.

She sucks in her cheeks. We used to have a good relationship when I was a kid. I wish we could find a way back to it, but she wanted better for her son and apparently I wasn't it. He was the golden boy who could do no wrong, and while I can't resent her for thinking that way, she blamed me for our teen pregnancy.

But she does love my boys.

"How's your dinner?" she asks Xander.

I clamp my lips together because Braden is much more diplomatic.

He shrugs. "It's alright."

She turns to Braden. "How about you?"

"It's good. Thanks."

I turn my head to look at Braden, but he shrugs just like his brother did and returns to eating.

"You two are talkative," Kay says.

"Eating," Braden mumbles with a mouth full of food.

I shake my head. They've been taught better.

"Anyone would think you didn't feed them, Chloe. They're starving."

"They're teenagers," I reply.

She fixes her gaze on me. "Scott never used to eat like this."

It's very rare for me to bite, but she pushes my buttons like no one else. "Scott used to eat like this all the time. And then we'd go out and he'd buy more food."

"You did always say Scott ate us out of house and home at times," Preston says.

Across the table, I meet Preston's eyes. He gives me a kind smile.

"Well, yes, but Braden and Xander seem hungry."

"They can eat a full meal and still be hungry. They're growing boys."

She huffs and returns to eating.

I'm not sure I'll ever be able to win her over, and if it was just me I wouldn't subject myself to her scrutiny.

It's exhausting, but at least it's only for one evening.

ELEVEN
HUNTER

CHLOE: *Dinner at six. Please join us.*

My head's been elsewhere since I got that text, and I've not focussed on work at all.

I poke my head out of my office. "Liz, can you take the interview at four for me? You've done all the paperwork for it. I trust you to decide if the guy's a good fit."

Her side-eye makes me chuckle. "You? Control-freak Hunter letting me decide who works here? What's wrong with you?"

I grin. She's right. I've had a tight control on staff intake since I started the company, and the best hire I ever made was she. But I've never given her a chance to spread her wings and maybe it's time to do that.

Liz has been with me from the beginning. She's about twenty years older, with her own grown-up family, and she was looking for an opportunity to run her own office. I've never regretted hiring her.

"Nothing's wrong. I just have another engagement."

Her eyebrows rise. "Is it a woman?"

Chuckling, I nod. "It's been a while, but yes. She's just a friend before you ask. Not that it's really any of your business."

"It never is. Good luck. I mean, you have to want to be more than friends if you're giving me hiring responsibility." She looks back down at the paperwork on her desk.

I smile and shake my head. "When did you take such an interest in my potential love life?"

She fixes her grey-eyed gaze on me. "You were such a pain in the arse after your divorce, and you've been grumpy ever since. Whether she's a friend or more, it's nice to see you behaving like an actual human."

All I can do is laugh again as I close the door and go back to my desk. She's right. Going through what I did made me harder than I'd like, but I wanted to protect myself. Maybe things are changing. Having Chloe back in my life in any way definitely makes everything better.

Another hour of working on these contracts, and I'll get home and ready for dinner with Chloe and her family. I'm still unhappy about what happened at Meredith's house. And if that Russell bloke gets anywhere near Chloe again, it'll be too soon.

He had no right to put his hands on a woman, and they'd literally just met. Even days later, thinking about it makes me mad.

And she's not just any woman, which makes it even more personal.

She's Chloe.

"JUST A MINUTE."

I smile at the sound of Chloe's voice, and even wider when she opens the door.

There's a spot of flour on her nose.

"Hunter."

"Hey, Chlo."

I reach out and brush the flour away. "You spilled something."

She laughs. "Thanks."

Something's different, but I can't quite put my finger on it. Chloe's cheeks are pink and her smile is even more luminescent than usual. She's right in front of me, but seems to be struggling to find anything to say. What's up with that?

I open my mouth.

"Hi." She blushes and looks down, and it's the cutest thing I think I've ever seen. This is not her usual reaction to me.

"I ... I got your message. What's up?"

Chloe smiles. "Xander made the first fifteen rugby team for his school. We're celebrating."

I grin. "That's fantastic."

Her eyes shine with excitement. "I thought we'd have a special dinner—Xander's choice, and he wanted to invite you."

"Really?" Xander's shown interest in talking to me at times, but out of the two, I thought he'd be the least likely to want me around.

"He knows you played in school." She takes my hand in hers and squeezes it. "And I might have suggested it in the first place."

My eyebrows rise. "Chloe Cooper, are you flirting with me?"

She hesitates, sucking on her bottom lip, which is the single most erotic thing I think I've ever seen.

"Maybe."

"I think maybe we need to talk about this."

She takes a step forward. "Maybe we do."

I reach for her, wrapping my hand around her wrist as I keep looking into her blue eyes. The aching need I feel for her seems to be reflected back at me. Is this real?

This has always been a one-way thing, but the changes in the way Chloe's looking at me, and the differences in her breathing as our gazes stay locked tell me that's no longer the case.

"I ... I don't know what this is, Hunter. But I know I like it." She raises her free hand to cup my cheek. "The other night stirred up feelings I thought were dead in me."

"What kind of feelings?"

She licks her lips. "Well ..."

"Mum, I got my jersey." Xander walks in holding a familiar looking shirt. His gaze falls to my hand on his mother's wrist and his smile disappears.

I let go of Chloe, and she drops her hand.

"When's dinner?" he asks, eyes now narrowed.

"About half an hour away. I just put the potatoes in to roast."

He chin lifts, eyeing me with the same suspicion he did from the start. I think Xander and I need to talk.

"Thanks, Mum." He narrows his gaze. "We're having *my* favourite."

"So I hear. Smells amazing. I can't wait."

His lips twitch. God, this kid is so much like his dad. But if he's that much like Scott, I know he's capable of a lot of love.

"Knock, knock."

I turn at the sound of a male voice.

"Uncle Caleb." Xander's face lights up. "Mum invited you?"

"Of course I did. Caleb played rugby too." Chloe fixes her gaze on me. "All the boys I knew did."

Caleb Baxter was never a part of our crowd, being a few years older than Chloe, and he takes a step in the door before he looks at me.

"Caleb, do you remember Hunter Emerson? Hunter, my big brother Caleb."

I extend my hand.

"Of course." He gives it a firm shake while eyeing me up and down. "You were Scott's friend?"

"I was. And Chloe's."

"Hunter lives next door," Chloe says.

"Does he now? It's good to meet you, Hunter."

Chloe kisses him on the cheek. "Dinner's about half an hour away. Grab a beer and get one for Hunter while you're at it."

"So bossy." He grins.

"Always. Now, get to it." Chloe slaps him on the arse with her tea towel.

He laughs and turns toward the fridge. “How on earth do Braden and Xander put up with you?”

“They love me.”

She walks over to the oven and opens it.

“Is that lamb?” I ask.

“It sure is. Mum cooked one the first night we were home, and—”

“You poor thing.” Caleb returns, handing me a beer. “I’m not sure how Mum manages to screw it up so badly every time.”

“Me neither.” Chloe says.

“Mum’s lamb is way better than Grandma’s.” Xander grins.

“I can’t wait to try it.”

Chloe closes the oven and turns to smile at me. I don’t miss that Caleb arches an eyebrow, but Xander seems oblivious.

I’m not even sure what she’s doing, but I like it.

DINNER IS AMAZING.

I don’t have much to do with my parents these days, but it brings back memories of the family dinners we used to share before their bitter divorce.

This is what it feels like to be a family.

Chloe and the boys share stories of their life before they moved here—stories her brother hasn’t heard either—and I’m lost in the laughter and love around the table.

She’s bringing me back to life without even knowing it.

I’ve been so dead since my own marriage breakup, but Chloe brings the sunshine as she always did.

“So, Hunter was Scott’s friend when you were kids?” Caleb says. “I’m sorry I don’t remember you, dude. I never paid that much attention to Chloe’s life back then.”

“I was. I met Scott when I started school.”

“So, how did you guys end up hanging out again?”

“The school reunion,” Chloe says. “I walked in and was so

thankful to see a familiar face. And then it turned out Hunter lived next door."

"Really? Now he can come over when you need help instead of you calling me from across town."

"Thanks a lot." She throws a napkin at him.

He laughs.

"I'm always around, and ready to help whenever you need it" I grin.

"Good to know." There's that smile again complete with the sparkle in her eyes, and for the second time Caleb glances between us. There's a tension that didn't seem to exist before, and I like it.

Caleb's chuckle is low, but I hear it.

And I have a smile of my own as Chloe keeps glancing at me.

"I'M STUFFED." I lean back and pat my stomach. "That was brilliant, Chlo."

"Glad you liked it."

After a full roast lamb dinner, she'd produced a Pavlova covered in whipped cream and berries. Xander's favourite.

"Thanks for choosing all that, Xander."

"I might have to come over for dinner more often," Caleb says.

"You know you're always welcome," Chloe says. She flicks her gaze to me. "You too."

"I'll remember that."

"Why don't you go and put your feet up while Hunter and I take care of the dishes," Caleb says.

Chloe glances between us. "It's just loading the dishwasher."

He nods. "I know. Just fuck off and let me get to know this guy."

She laughs, shaking her head. "Fine. I know where I'm not wanted. I've got some washing to fold upstairs anyway."

I watch as she heads up the stairs behind the boys while Caleb opens the dishwasher.

Together, we stack the dishes, working quickly and quietly. Clearly, something's on Caleb's mind as he seems to study me.

"I've been encouraging Chloe to find a little romance in her life. Is that going to be you?"

"I ..." I hesitate and nearly drop a plate. "I'd like it to be."

"Good." He leans against the cupboards and crosses his arms over his chest. "You have to be important to her to get an invite tonight. Xander will be the tough one to crack if you stick around."

His words catch me by surprise. "I worked that one out for myself."

"They've all been through a lot. If you pursue her, you take really good care of her or you'll have me to answer to."

I nod. "Understood."

"You seem like a good guy, Hunter. She just needs someone to love her, and not mess her around. Chloe's already been through enough."

"Agreed. Hurting her is the last thing I ever want to do."

For a moment, we're locked in place as his gaze doesn't let up. Getting Caleb onside has to be an advantage. He clearly adores his sister, and he's not going to hesitate to get in my way if he decides I'm not enough for Chloe.

"Seriously, dude. Sweep her off her feet. Scott loved her, but they were an old married couple when they were kids. Give her the world."

I swallow hard. This is more than just his approval. He's encouraging me to do this, and I want this so badly, I'll give her everything she needs. There's no point in holding anything back.

"That's what I want to do."

He smiles and closes the dishwasher door. "That's all I need to hear. Don't get me wrong. Scott was a solid guy, and he loved the shit out of her. But she missed out on so much, and I think she deserves it."

"I agree."

Chloe walks into the room with Xander. "Are you guys done?"

"Done and I'm out of here. Be good, boys. Might visit at the weekend for a swim." He winks at Chloe. "Congratulations, Xander. Your dad would be proud." Turning to me, he smiles. "Good to meet you, Hunter."

"You too."

My heart's singing at him giving me his blessing to pursue something with Chloe. I don't need it, but having her family's backing is reassuring.

"Goodnight, Uncle Caleb." Xander turns to Chloe. "I'm going to my room. Thanks for the dinner, Mum." He kisses her on the cheek. "See ya later, Hunter."

"Have a good night, dude."

I even get a smile out of him as he passes me and heads up the stairs.

CALEB'S LONG GONE, leaving Chloe and me standing in the kitchen.

"I should probably go too."

Chloe's lips twitch. "You don't have to yet."

"I've got work in the morning. I left my office manager to do some hiring today because I was invited elsewhere."

She nods. "I have work too. I'm behind on where I wanted to be on my word count, so I should really buckle down tomorrow."

"Goodnight, Chloe."

I step toward her and run my thumb down her cheek. The urge to kiss her is so strong, but this is a woman who was devastated by the loss of her husband. If I'm going to explore this with her, I need to take it slow.

"Goodnight."

When I was a teenager, I'd have killed to see the affectionate look in her eyes she has now.

I have to go now, or I'll do something I could regret.

We're frozen, just looking at each other, but it's not awkward. It's like a new understanding blossoming between us. Does she want me to chase her?

For now I'll go home, but this is in no way over.

In fact, it's just begun.

TWELVE
HUNTER

CHLOE: *Thank you for last night.*

Me: *You're welcome. Let's do it again. Soon.*

I want dinner with Chloe every night. I just want her and everything that comes with.

It's mid-week when I've had enough of work. Liz has managed to get Gary to see a counsellor, but I'm still not sure it's enough. At least he's coming to work sober.

Chloe's been on my mind the whole time, and I want to know if I'm on hers.

I'm halfway home when I spot the pizza place. It's still early.

Sweep her off her feet.

Caleb's words ring in my ears. Does turning up with dinner count?

I pull into the car park and head in into the store. If Braden and Xander eat anything like I did as a teenager, we'll need a lot of food. I'm not sure what the boys like, but given the way they dug into the steak and potatoes meal, I order meaty pizzas.

There's a bottle store next door, so while I'm waiting, I walk over to buy a couple of bottles of sparkling wine.

Just making this decision is settling. I want so much to win her over, and if pizza helps buy my way into those boys' hearts then it's a small price to pay.

With the food, I drive home, pulling into my driveway and grabbing it before heading over next door.

Balancing the pizza boxes in one hand, and the wine bottles in the other, I use my foot to knock on the door.

Chloe's eyes widen as she pulls it open. "What are you doing?"

"I have pizza. Thought you might like a night off from cooking."

Chloe grins. "That's so sweet."

I loop past her and into the kitchen where I place the boxes on the table. "Don't tell people I'm sweet. They'll think I have a soft side."

She picks up a pizza box and opens it, taking a deep breath. "Oh, I know you have a soft side. But your secret is safe with me. This is heavenly."

One of the boys, and at first I'm not sure which one, bounds down the stairs. "Is that pizza?" His eyes grow wide at the four boxes.

"Hunter brought us dinner. Can you go and get your brother?"

"Sure."

She turns back to me. "Thank you. I really appreciate this."

"I know you're on a deadline."

Her lips curl. "That's very considerate of you."

"Told you I'm here for you, Chlo."

Happiness radiates from her. Something's definitely shifted between us, and maybe tonight I'll make my move.

"Braden said there's pizza here?" Xander appears in the doorway.

Chloe turns to smile at him. "Yes. Hunter thought we might like it."

He lifts his chin toward me. "Thanks, Hunter."

"You're welcome, bud."

"Chloe, I grabbed some wine for later if you'd like." I hold up the bag.

"That would be lovely." She smiles. "Red or white?"

"Bubbly. Want me to put it in the fridge?"

"That'd be great."

She grabs plates out of the cupboard and places them on the table. "How about we all just help ourselves?"

"I got plenty because I know you have two growing boys to feed."

"Oh, I do. It's never ending with the way those two are growing like beanstalks. Thank you."

We all hang back while Chloe grabs some slices, before the boys and I pick from the selection and sit.

Braden's the one who talks. He talks about the house, and about school—he even talks about his dad. Xander's quiet.

Chloe seems to retreat, her smile fading as the meal goes on.

We eat until we're full, but she's back to picking at her meal.

"Did you have a good day?" I ask.

She doesn't make eye contact, but bows her head. "It was quiet, and I caught up on some writing. I'm just a little tired."

Her tone is flat, and un-Chloe-like.

"Sorry to hear that."

Silence falls over the table, and the boys exchange a glance I don't understand.

"We'll clean up, Mum." Braden stands and kisses Chloe on the cheek.

"Thank you. I'm sorry to cut this short, but I really need to lie down."

I frown. "Are you okay?"

She nods. "I'll be fine."

Chloe stands and leaves the room without even saying goodbye. Given how close we've been growing, it's not like her at all. She seems unsettled.

"What just happened?" I look first at one boy, then the other.

Braden sucks on his bottom lip.

"It's the anniversary of Dad's death," Xander says.

I blink, rapidly, and sit back in my seat. "Chloe didn't say anything. Shit. I should have known."

Braden shakes his head. "It's okay. Thank you for tonight, though. I think it's what we needed."

"Yeah, it was pretty cool."

I shift my gaze to Xander. "That's praise coming from you."

He grins, pushes his chair out, and stands. "I'll clear away the rubbish and then head up to my room."

The bottle of wine I brought sits unopened on the bench. "Where are your wine glasses?"

Braden points across the room. "That cupboard."

"I might take the wine to your mum and see how she's doing."

He shoots me a wary look.

"Your mum means a lot to me. Always did. And you guys do too. If there's anything either of you ever want to talk about, I'm here. Okay?"

Braden nods, and when I shift my gaze to Xander, he raises his eyebrows in acknowledgement.

"I'm sorry your dad isn't here. I always thought we'd meet up again some day. But I'm really glad I've met the two of you, and I hope we can be friends."

"I'd like that," Braden says.

Xander grunts. There's still a long way to go with him, but if he's as stubborn as his father ...

Trudging over to the cupboard, Xander retrieves two wine glasses and then hands them to me.

I raise an eyebrow and then scruff his dark hair. "Thanks."

He huffs out a "sure."

Leaving them to clean up, I make my way toward Chloe's bedroom and tap on the bedroom door.

"Chloe?"

"You can open it," she calls.

Turning the handle, I push open the door then close it behind me after entering the room.

She's lying on the bed, and her brows knit as I approach.

"Are you okay?"

Chloe shrugs. "I will be."

I sit on the bed. "Why didn't you tell me what today was?"

She sniffs and sucks on her bottom lip for a moment. "I didn't want to kill your mood. You turned up at just the right time and were just what I needed. And having a family dinner with you was so good."

I lean over and run my thumb down her cheek. "It was. But I can't be there for you if you don't let me."

"I'm sorry."

I shake my head. "You never have to apologise. Today must have been hard."

"It was, but you made it better." Her smile is small, but it's there. "Thank you for everything."

"You're welcome. But I thought I could make tonight better, and we didn't drink the wine."

Chloe smiles. "You're right. We didn't."

"So, I brought it with me." I hold up the bottle and two glasses.

She laughs. "I'm not sure if that's a good idea. I don't react well to wine."

"In what way?"

Her eyes flash with mischief. "It either puts me to sleep or makes me horny, and I can't cope with one of those."

"Even if I volunteer to be tribute?"

Her laughter on this day of all days warms my heart. "I love being around you, Hunter. You always make me feel better."

"I'll take that as a compliment and pour us both a drink, then."

"You do that."

She props herself up on the pillows as I pour the bubbly liquid and then hand her a glass.

"To Scott." I say as I hold up mine.

She clinks her glass with mine. "To Scott."

We take our first sip in silence, and I climb up on the bed properly, sitting next to her.

Chloe runs her index finger around the rim of her glass. "I miss him. I know it's been a long time now, but there's a big part of me that just wants him to walk back through the door."

I look down at my wine glass, pausing before looking back up. "I bet. And I'm sure that'll never change." I take another sip of my drink. "I wish I'd been able to say goodbye."

Tears fill her eyes. "I wish I had too. But the last conversation we had, I told him I love him, and I have to make do with that."

As a tear rolls down her cheek, I place my free hand over hers. "That was everything to him. He worshipped the ground you walked on. If that was the last thing he heard from you, then he would have died a happy man."

She sniffs. "Do you think so?"

"I know so. He loved you so very much, and that never stopped all the time I knew him." I smile. "A lifetime isn't enough for a love like that."

Chloe smiles and downs the rest of her drink in one hit.

"More please."

"Oh, you're just going to be trouble tonight, aren't you?"

She laughs. "I'll try not to be."

I grab the wine bottle and refill her glass. "You know Scott would never have approved to me sitting in bed alone with you."

"No, he wouldn't." She takes another sip. "That never changed, you know? Right until the end he put me first. The kids, too, but I never had a day when I felt unloved." Tears fill her eyes again. "It's so stupid crying about it. That should make me happy."

"It's not stupid. And you know wherever he is, he still loves you. Always will."

She takes another long drink.

"Sometimes I feel like I should have moved on by now. But then it doesn't feel right." She looks at me from under her eyelashes.

"You'll know when you're ready."

Chloe sighs before downing the rest of her drink.

"You need to slow down." I laugh.

"I was never a big drinker. But this is nice. Maybe it's time for me to do things I've never done before." She runs her tongue along her lower lip.

My cock twitches. "Like what?"

"Get really drunk. Bungee jump. Go skydiving. I don't know." She holds her glass out. "Start by topping me up."

"When did you get so bossy?"

"When I became a mum." She laughs.

I chuckle and refill her glass again. The bottle's disappearing quickly, and I've barely had any of it. I take a sip.

"Want to get drunk with me?" she asks. "I kinda skipped that whole phase. By the time I was old enough to buy alcohol, I was breastfeeding twins."

My heart lurches. Caleb was right. Chloe has missed out on a lot. And while I'm sure she wouldn't want to give up a thing, it's not fair to try and tie her down before she's spread her wings.

"It'll take more than this to get me drunk."

She swirls her glass. "I used to envy Scott. He was such a good dad and an amazing husband, but he had so much more freedom than I did. I ... I was at home with the twins and he got to leave the house every day. But we were happy." Her brows twitch as tears well in her eyes. "Damn it. I didn't want to cry."

"It's my fault."

Chloe shakes her head. "No. I would have done it one way or another. I'm just glad you're here."

I reach out and wipe her tears away with my fingers. "I'm glad I am too. I don't want you going through this alone."

"I'm never alone while I have my boys." She's slurring a little, but there's a faint smile on her lips.

I scan her expression. "That's true. They're such great kids, Chloe. You did good."

She drains her drink.

"Should I get the other bottle, or ...?" I ask.

I'm not sure if it's a good idea, but it's clear she needs to talk and this is working to get it out of her.

"Yes, please. I think it's just what I need tonight."

Her eyes are hazy, and something tells me she'll be asleep before too long. But she's inside her own home and safe, and leaving her alone for tonight of all nights doesn't sit well on me.

"I'll be back in a minute."

The rest of the house is quiet. It sounds like the boys have retreated to their own rooms, and I hesitate outside their closed doors. I'll check in with them in the morning how they are. Today will be tough on them too.

I haven't even stopped to think about how I feel.

But none of that is important when the people I love are in pain. And I do love them.

I retrieve the wine bottle from the fridge and grab a bag of potato chips. It's not much, but maybe this'll lessen the blow for Chloe tomorrow.

She beams when I walk back into the room. Her blonde hair's mussed up from lying back on the pillows, and her cheeks are pink as is the end of her nose. I've never seen her drunk before. And while I think she's a ways off that, she's well on the path.

I throw the bag of chips on the bed. "Hungry?"

"Ravenous." She licks her lips. "At least no one else is going to complain about crumbs in the bed."

She laughs like it's the funniest joke ever.

"I'm not sure you should have any more to drink, Chlo."

"If you don't fill up my glass, Hunter, I'll drink the whole bottle by myself."

I laugh. "I'm keeping an eye on you, young lady."

"Good. I like that idea." She holds up her glass and bites her lip, her eyes heavy and locked with mine.

I have the urge to lean forward and take her in my arms, but I've got to know if she longs for me and only me, like I long for her.

I fill up our glasses, place the bottle on the bedside cabinet and lie on the bed beside her. "I wish I'd known about Scott. I would have been there for you."

She steadies her gaze on me. "You're here now."

"I know, but ..." I play my bottom lip between my teeth. "It doesn't feel like it's enough."

"It's enough." She drains her glass.

"Steady on." I laugh.

"Call it Dutch courage."

"For what?" I take a sip of my own glass before leaning back to place it next to the bottle. "You can tell me anything, Chloe."

"Do you—" she holds her glass out. "—know what else I missss?" Chloe blinks, her eyelids heavy as she tries to focus on my face.

I have a feeling she won't feel well in the morning, but my guess is talking for her is therapeutic—it has been for me.

"What?"

"The sex. I miss having a sex life. And I've had offers, but I can't do it. I almost wish I could, but I need to feel something more than just wanting sex."

My mouthful of drink goes down the wrong way, and I cough before choking out the words. "I can understand that."

"I just want to love and be loved again. But it's hard." She licks her lips. "And then there's you."

It's hard not to smile, but I need to know more about what she means. "Me?"

"You were unexpected, Hunter Emerson. You've been sneaking into my heart, and I don't have a clue what to do about it." She drops her empty glass onto the carpet beside the bed before lying on her back with her arms above her head.

"Is that right?" I'm not sure she's in any position to tell me this right now, but it's what my heart needs to hear. "What did I do to deserve that?"

She reaches up to run her fingers through my beard. "Just by being you. I can't remember what it's like to fall in love, but you are doing all the right things. I think." Her eyelids flicker, and it's obvious she's fighting sleep. "I like the way I feel around you."

"You're easy to love, Chloe. So, so easy."

"Then stay the night and love me."

For a moment, I examine her expression closely.

"Chloe, I ..."

"I want you, Hunter."

THIRTEEN

CHLOE

I THINK I just told Hunter that I had feelings for him.

But it's hard to tell what I'm saying out loud versus what's in my head. Wine is always the worst.

My eyelids grow heavier, and I wriggle down in the bed. Hunter lies down beside me.

"Roll over," he says.

I roll onto my side, and he pulls me up against him, my back to his chest. Without another word, he tangles his fingers in mine and rests our joined hands on my stomach.

And that's the last thing I remember.

I SWEAR, all it takes is a glass or two of wine and I'm on my arse for the night. I don't care that I'm a lightweight when it comes to drinking, and I've never been one to indulge, but last night was a reminder of the worst night of my life.

I let out a contented sigh at the warmth on my back, and the arm draped over me. *Hunter*. He took such good care of me, and I was so glad for his company on a night that's always difficult to get through.

I'm just going to lie here and enjoy his presence for as long as I can.

His body's curled around me, his thighs pressed against mine, and if I'm not mistaken ... My eyes fly open. It's been a long time since I've had a man in my bed, and some things are always the same.

He murmurs as I pull away a little, roll over, and look at him.

I'd know Hunter anywhere, but he's changed so much since we were kids. It seems weird to think of him as a man instead of the boy we left behind.

And he is all man.

I place my palms on his abdomen. He's warm to the touch, and solid underneath that shirt. Curious, I bite my bottom lip as I raise the hem and tuck my hands underneath, palm to his skin.

Part of me hates that I'm so innocent in some ways. I was with only one man for years, so Hunter's like forbidden fruit that I know absolutely nothing about. I'm well aware of my naivety when it comes to things like dating, and to be honest, men in general.

But Hunter's become not only the man I have a crush on, but also my rock. I have no doubt that when he says he'll always be here for me—he means it.

I explore his abs with my fingertips, and slowly walk them up to his pecs. His chest hair feels funny beneath my fingers, but it just increases his appeal. He's not what I'm used to. He's undoubtedly Hunter.

"What *are* you doing?" There's bemusement in his voice.

I drop my hands, but one of his closes over one of mine and pulls it back to his chest.

"I didn't tell you to stop."

Stay the night and love me.

Wait. Did I really say that? My cheeks blaze.

"I like you touching me."

My heart pounds as I flatten my palm and slide it downward.

"Chloe." His strained tone tells me he's as affected by me as I am by him.

My hands reach the waistband of his pants.

He shakes his head.

Hunter's eyes seem so dark as he skims his thumb across my bottom lip.

"Our first time together isn't going to be rushed. We'll take it slow. But you have to be ready, and I'm not doing this while you still need to sleep off the night before."

"I'm fine," I whisper.

"You look tired, and I bet anything your head is thumping. Am I right?"

I feel petulant as I pout and nod.

He raises my chin with his fingers and brushes his lips against mine. "Get some sleep. We'll talk later."

I know he's right as I yawn. It's been a long time since I've slept as well as I did last night beside him, but I'm still feeling awful.

Hunter rolls off the bed as I close my eyes and drift off to dream of him.

"MUM, Hunter said you'd need these."

I open an eye to see Braden standing over me, a glass of water in one hand, and two white pills in his other palm.

"Thank you," I croak.

Sitting up, I hold out my hand and he drops the pills into it, handing me the water at the same time.

"I don't think I've ever seen you like this."

I chuckle. "It's been a while since I've had that much to drink."

"Yesterday was a bad day. I'm glad you're okay."

I swallow down the pills and grimace. "I'll be fine."

"Are you with Hunter now?"

His eyes betray his anxiety. It took so long for us to adjust to a new normal. Any relationship I enter will be a big deal for all of us.

"No. Would you be okay if I was?"

His nod is slight, but his face drops all its tension. "I like him. You're different now he's around. Yesterday was a bad day for you, but you were laughing and smiling. That makes me happy."

I reach out and take his hand in mine. "I'm glad to hear it. It's time we all had some happiness in our lives."

"Xander might not feel the same way."

Sighing, I lie back on my pillows. "Well, nothing is happening right now, so he has some time to adjust. I have a lot of thinking to do."

"Do you want to know what I like about Hunter?"

I smile. "Tell me."

"The way he looks at you. It's the way Dad used to. He doesn't want to be Dad, but he's there for me and Xander."

I nod. "He's a good man."

"I guess that's the long way of saying that I'm okay with you and Hunter." He pushes his floppy fringe out of his eyes, and the simple action takes my breath away.

"You are so your father's son."

He screws up his nose. "What do you mean?"

"You're a lot like him. Xander is too, obviously, but in different ways. He'd be really proud of you."

"Do you think so?"

"He loved you before you were born. I know so."

His smile warms my heart. He sits on the bed.

"You two were so young. Was he happy about me and Xan?"

I nod. "You were a surprise. Even more so when we found out there were two of you. But your dad and I always knew we wanted to be together forever. And you and Xander made our little family complete."

There's so much more I want to say, but I'm not sure how he'll take it. Like how Scott passed out the moment he realised we were having two babies. I might have done the same if I wasn't already lying down.

We both knew all our plans were out the window. But we pulled together and found our way through.

I was never meant to be left alone.

"I love you, Mum." Braden leans forward and hugs me.

"I love you too. I guess I'd better get out of bed and take you to school."

He shakes his head. "Hunter's got that covered. If that's okay."

I nod. "It's fine. Have a good day."

As he leaves, he passes Xander who's standing in the doorway.

"Do you really have a hangover?"

I laugh. "I do. First one in forever."

He screws up his face. "Can we take the leftover pizza for lunch?"

"You can do whatever you want today."

His smile looks so much like Scott's it makes my heart ache. "Okay. Hope you're feeling better soon, Mum."

And then I'm glad he closes the door because it's all I can do to hold in my tears until it's closed.

I DON'T EVEN REMEMBER FALLING asleep. But my phone chiming to remind me it's time for the school pick up leaves me groaning.

I've slept all day.

I'm not even sure I can remember the last time I did that.

Sighing, I force myself to sit up and pick up the phone. The screen's bright and blurry, but I turn the alarm off.

There's a text.

Hunter: *I told the boys I'll pick them up. Don't worry about them. Just rest.*

Me: *Thank you*

Hunter: *The ball's in your court, Chloe. I'm ready whenever you are. You just have to say the word.*

Despite my throbbing head pain, I smile.

Hunter: *And make sure you drink plenty of water.*

I laugh. Hunter wants to be with me.

Last night, I think I threw myself at him, but he didn't take advantage. And now he's basically telling me he's prepared to wait.

I just have to get up the courage without the alcohol and tell him how I feel.

How the hell do I get brave enough to do that?

FOURTEEN

HUNTER

IT'S hard to bide my time waiting for Chloe, but at this point I need her to come to me rather than chase after her.

She needs to be ready, and I know we're close, but the jury's still out on how far I can push. As it is, I've laid my cards on the table and now it's her turn.

Her move ends up being so subtle, I almost miss it.

It's been two days since I left her in her bed, sleeping off the night before. My body still remembers what it was like to have her hands on me, and her gentle exploration gives me hope.

She told me she wanted me, but I want her to say it when she's sober.

It's hard to fight the urge to just go after what I want, but she's not going anywhere. We can take our time. There's still a big part of me that can't believe she's back in my life and that, this time, I have a chance with her. We've both been through tough times, and now maybe we can start a new life together.

It's after eleven when I look out the window. Chloe's in her bikini, lying on a lounger by the pool, and soaking up the rays of the full moon.

I grin. She even has her sunglasses on. And then I watch as she dips her glasses, looks toward my house, and slips them back on again.

If she's not trying to get my attention, then I have no idea what she's doing, but I fully intend to find out.

I walk downstairs and open the back door. We still haven't talked about fixing the fence, and for now it's an easy way to get onto her property. Crossing the lawn, I push open the pool gate and approach her.

"What *are* you doing?"

She removes her glasses. "It's a warm night, and the boys are both asleep. I thought I'd come out and enjoy the pool."

"You haven't been near the pool. You're not wet."

Chloe's smug smile nearly brings me to my knees. "I'm not sure how you can tell when you're that far away."

I narrow my gaze. "Chloe Cooper. Are you flirting with me again?"

"Oh, I think we're well past that. We were the other night, but you turned me down."

Taking another few steps closer, I drop to kneel beside her. "Did you finish off that wine?"

"No. Nothing to drink tonight. My head's clear."

I scan her expression. She's so damn beautiful out here in the moonlight. I want her so much I could burst.

"Aren't you worried about the boys waking up?"

She shakes her head. "Their rooms aren't near the back of the house. And they've got school tomorrow, so they won't be up until seven."

I chuckle. "I like this side of you."

"Which side?"

"The side that's brought you out here."

She reaches for my arm. "You know this isn't usually me. And I can't believe I'm doing this, but I wanted to make it clear how I felt without actually saying the words."

"Tell me what you want, Chloe. I need to hear it from you."

She licks her lips. "I told you what I want. I want you."

"Could have just come over today and told me that."

"But I *need* you to make the first move. I'm afraid to."

Her expression falters in my stunned silence. I shouldn't be so surprised, but she wasn't sober when she propositioned me. Now she is, and ready to admit it.

I cock my head. "You were the one with her hands all over me the other morning."

"You were the one who slept in my bed."

I blow out a breath and shrug. "You got me there."

"Thank you for taking care of me." Her tone softens.

"I'll always look out for you from now on. No matter what happens between us."

She blinks slowly. "So, what is happening between us?"

I lean closer. "Well, there's no way I'm missing my chance with you. You're stuck with me."

She's never looked at me the way she's doing so now, a look of wonder and longing all in one. "I wouldn't want to be without you. And you know how I feel now I've opened my big mouth."

I chuckle. "I'm glad you did. Made me realise this wasn't one-sided." Leaning closer until our faces are inches apart, I don't miss her sharp intake of breath. "Remind me what you want again?"

For a moment, she studies me, her breathing becoming more ragged. "You. I want you."

She whimpers as I claim her mouth with mine, my tongue skirting over hers as I finally kiss the woman I'm in love with. Twenty years I feel I've waited for this moment, from the time I realised I felt more than just friendship for her.

Chloe slides her hands up my face, cupping my cheeks as I kiss her deeply.

Her eyes are closed when we pull apart, and when she opens them again, I drown in the depth of her emotion. She's never looked at me the way she does now, but now I know what it's like to be loved by her. Or at least on the way to that.

Her lips twitch, and she reaches down to stroke my cock through my pants. I hitch an eyebrow.

"That's the second time you've done that. Are you sure you're ready?"

"I want to be with you."

"Chloe," I whisper.

She grabs hold of my head and pulls me back to kiss her. It's long and lingering and if my heart wasn't already hers, I'd be gone.

Chloe gasps as I drop my lips to her neck, planting soft kisses. She runs her hand over my shoulder and down my arm, gripping my bicep.

All I can smell is her lip gloss.

For such a subtle scent, it's indelibly her and burned into my brain. From the moment I saw her apply it at that dinner table, I've had the urge to taste it.

Now I have.

Now it's mine.

I tug down one side of her bikini top, exposing her rounded breast. She lets out a moan as I tease her nipple with my tongue, running her hands through my hair.

"You," she whispers.

I raise my head. "Me?"

Her eyes are so dark in the moonlight, but I see the wonder in them. "You're not the boy I remember."

I chuckle. "Oh, no, sweetheart. I'm so much more."

"I can see that." She bites her bottom lip. "I never expected to find this. All I wanted to do was come home."

"I'm glad you made that decision. I feel like my life's been in limbo, and now you're here ..." Her smile warms my heart, and she gasps into my mouth as I kiss her.

"I feel the same way."

"Are you sure you're ready for this? I know it's been a while, but ..."

"You mean a lot to me. I want more than sex."

"Whew." I grin.

"Speaking of ..." Her lips curl, and I kiss her hard until she lets go of my arm.

Returning to her breast, I slide my hand down her stomach. She sucks it in at my touch, and she trembles when I dip my hand into her bikini bottoms.

Her sharp intake of breath as I slide my finger over her clit leaves me smiling against her skin.

"Are you really ready for me?" I ask.

"I want this. I want you." She arches her back, and this beautiful woman who's so full of love and need enraptures me all over again.

And I'm the man she's chosen to give it all to.

I'm the man who'll guard her heart.

She rocks against my fingers as I divide my time between her lips and her breasts.

"Please, Hunter." She moans.

"What do you need?"

"I need to come."

I stroke her face, looking into her eyes. "Come with me, Chloe. Give it to me."

Her eyes never leave mine, but her face ... That look of absolute pleasure I only ever want her to have with me. She arches her back again, her body tensing before she lets out a long, loud moan.

"That's it, sweetheart. Feel better now?"

Her satisfied smile tells me all I need to know.

She laughs, leaning over and burying her face in my chest.

"This is just the start."

"I want more," she whispers.

I slide her bikini bottoms down her legs and fling them onto the ground.

"Are you sure?"

"Stop asking me that."

I chuckle. "Well, okay."

She spreads her legs, and I grin. "This is very forward of you, Chloe Cooper."

I slide a finger into her, and her gasp is so loud I'm pretty sure the neighbours would have heard it.

Her pussy's hot and wet, and my cock leaps to life as I tease her with my finger.

"Hunter." She gasps.

"Is this what you need?"

She nods. I bend my head to taste her. How do I tell her I once dreamed of this? I was younger, and wouldn't have known what to do, but there was a time when I wanted her as badly as I do now.

And now I have the chance to make her mine.

"Oh my God." She bucks beneath my tongue, and I get lost in pleasing her. It's all about Chloe right now, and giving her everything she needs.

The way she's wriggling around, we're going to collapse this damn lounger if I don't move her.

"I'm taking you home."

She laughs, softly. "Which home?"

"Mine. We don't want to disturb the boys with the amount of noise you'll be making."

I scoop her into my arms and carry her toward the fence and through the gate. Thankful I didn't close the back door, I carry her through and up the stairs direct to my bedroom. She clings to me the whole way, burying her face in my neck.

"Hunter," she whispers.

I lower her onto the bed, take a step back, and rake my eyes over Chloe Copper, naked and ready for me. "Are you really ready for this?"

She nods. "I need you."

I tug my shirt off, and Chloe's eyes widen. She lets out a loud sigh, and my eyebrows rise. "What?"

"You just look ..." Her cheeks flush pink. "This is going to sound silly."

I crawl up the bed. I'm well aware that I'm not like the boy she knew before she left. The bulked-up man before her is nothing like I used to be.

"Tell me."

"You're beautiful."

I grin, lying beside her and cupping her head to pull her to me for a kiss.

"How so?"

She reaches out to touch my chest. "No. This is really dumb. We're both thirty-five years old and not children anymore."

"Nothing's dumb." I kiss her again. "I want to know what's going on in that head of yours."

"Seeing you is different to touching you." She licks her lips. "Although, I want to do a lot more of that."

I chuckle.

"It's just that you're so grown up. We all are, but you ... I don't really know how to explain it."

"I shaved my chest hair once. If you'd prefer it, I could ..."

"Don't you dare. I love it the way it is. It's very you." Her blue eyes scan mine. "You're just not what I was used to, and I like it." Chloe's lips twitch. "I mean I *really* like it."

"All I want to do is make you happy."

She looks into my eyes then kisses me.

I love Chloe. There's lightness in my heart that's not been there for a very long time, and I don't ever want to lose it. It's like all the years in between never happened and we're here as we're meant to be. We can't forget the past, but maybe we can put it behind us and find our future together.

"You're doing a good job so far."

"Now. Where were we?"

She drops her knees apart, and I move between them.

"Don't be shy about asking me for what you want."

"It's not easy."

I reach up and link my fingers in hers, pinning her hands to the bed, dropping my head down beside hers.

"It's me, Chlo. It's Hunter. You can trust me."

Her breath is soft against my cheek. "I know. It's just ..."

I bend down and lick her pussy until she arches off the bed again.

"That. Please."

I chuckle as I go back down on her again, teasing her until she cries out her release to my empty bedroom.

Crawling across the bed, I pull out a condom from my bedside cabinet. Chloe watches me wide-eyed as I roll it on.

This is it.

Tonight she's made all my dreams come true, and I just hope I can do the same for her.

I lean forward when she reaches for me.

"Don't treat me like I'm made of china." She strokes my hair. "I've been thinking about this, and I don't want you to be gentle."

"I'm not sure you know what you're asking of me."

Chloe smiles. "I want to spend tomorrow remembering tonight."

"Chloe, I ..."

"I won't break."

Her eyes shine with happiness, and all I want to do is give my girl exactly what she wants.

I sink into her waiting body, and close my eyes as she clenches around me. I think I'm in heaven, she feels so good.

Opening my eyes, I watch her as I start to move. She's got a look of concentration on her face that fades every so often as she loses herself to the rhythm. Her lips are parted, and she breathes heavily as I lean over her.

I suck her bottom lip, and she thrusts her hips to meet me. The air's filled with the wet, slapping sounds of sex, and the scent of her.

"Are you okay?" I ask.

She nods, spreading her legs a little wider. I drive in deep but not too hard. She said she wants to still feel me tomorrow, but I'm still a little afraid of breaking her. While she's not fragile, I'm not sure she can take all I can give her.

"More."

Though, I could be wrong.

"Flip over."

Without any hesitation, she rolls over as soon as I pull out of her. She raises herself up on her knees, bending over a little to give me access.

I slide back into her, gripping her by the breasts and thrusting again. Her moan and the way she arches her back tell a story all in itself. I take her hard and fast, not pausing to ask how she's doing. She's telling me that in the way she's practically purring at my actions.

"Hunter."

My body tightens, and my release hits me so hard. She cries out again as I hold her tight against me, maybe a little too tight.

"What was that?" Her eyes are wide as I pull out of her and she turns back to face me.

"That was insane. I don't think I've ever come that hard."

I relax my grip, but she places her hands over mine.

"I did that?"

Lowering her gently onto the bed, I move as she rolls onto her back.

She smiles. "Well, how about that?"

"You're so proud of yourself."

"That was worth waiting for." She chuckles, but she has no idea.

In the past, I didn't even have the imagination for what we just did. Living it exceeds any expectations I ever had.

"I need to get rid of this condom. I'll be back in a minute. Use the en-suite if you need to. I'll go and use the main bathroom."

I give her a tender kiss, and her contented smile tells me everything I need to know about how she feels.

By the time I get back, she's rolled onto her side away from me, the sheet pulled up under her armpits.

And she's quiet. Which, isn't surprising—there'll be a lot going on in that head of hers.

I slide into bed beside her, drop my arm over her waist and kiss the back of her neck. "You okay?"

"I ... I'm fine."

"You don't get to 'I'm fine' me, Chloe Cooper. Tonight was a big thing for you. I'd have to be completely devoid of feeling not to know that. And you know that's far from me where you're concerned."

She drops her hand and links her fingers in mine. "I don't have any regrets about us, if that's what you're thinking."

"I know you don't have any complaints from the sounds you were making." I chuckle.

Chloe laughs. "No complaints at all. You were wonderful."

I plant a kiss on her shoulder. "I'm sure it's just weird to have sex with someone new after all these years."

She nods. "It was different."

"Different good? Different better?"

Chloe rolls onto her back, her smile reassuring and caring. "It's not a competition."

"You know how competitive I am." I know I'm pushing it, but it's amusing her, and right now that's how I help her get through this. "I need to know I'm the best you ever had."

Her laughter fills my bedroom, and it sounds so damn good. "I can't comment. But I can tell you that I enjoyed every second, and we might have to do it again to see if it was a fluke or not."

My mouth falls open. "You think me making you come that hard was a fluke?"

She shrugs. "Could be. There's only one way to find out."

I'M NOT sure I'll ever get enough of this.

To be with this woman who I know so well that even the years apart seem to have faded away.

Right now it's just Chloe and me, and nothing else matters.

"I love being in your arms," she murmurs.

I hold her tight and kiss her temple. She's where she's supposed to be, and I'm sure of that. Just as I'm sure of my feelings for her. And after tonight, it's clear she's along for this ride with me.

Closing my eyes, I still can't quite believe she's here, but she's in my arms and all is right in my world.

I'm not sure how much later I'm roused from sleep when she kisses my cheek, her breath hot against my skin.

"See you later."

"Where are you going?" I mumble.

"Home. Before the boys wake up."

I shake myself awake. "What? Why? Stay."

"I can't. Not yet." She leans over and kisses me.

I wrap my hand around her wrist, a little deflated at her leaving. "You don't want anyone knowing about us."

Chloe bites her bottom lip. "Just for a little while. We need to ease the boys into it."

"They're nearly adults, Chlo. They know me."

She tilts her head. "They do, but it's been a long, hard road back to what we have now. Xander, in particular, struggled with depression, and he's the one I worry about the most."

I take in what she says. She's right. They're still kids, and if I'm going to be with their mother, I need both of them to accept me. Chloe will always put them first, as she should.

"You give me butterflies when I can't remember having them before. I get so nervous around you, and I don't know why because, before we left town, I knew you my whole life." She sucks on her bottom lip. "I want this. I want you. But apart from my boys, I want to just have *us* to myself for a little while."

Her eyes are so full of concern, that I can see this is a big thing for her. Of course it is. I'm the first man in her life for four years, and those boys need to know that I love their mother and that I'll be there for them.

"Hunter, I became a mother at eighteen. I've not had a real moment to myself since." She looks up at the ceiling. "I love my family, but this is my chance to experience so many things I never did without any extra pressure. Maybe I'm being selfish, but I can't remember falling in love the first time around. I want that."

As she moves her gaze back to me, I lean in and kiss her softly. "Then that's what we'll do. I already feel like I waited my whole life for you. What's a few extra days."

Her lips quirk. "Days?"

"Hours. How quickly can I get you to fall in love with me?"

Chloe smiles. "You have no idea what you do to me. It terrifies me but feels so good."

"Tell me."

Her lips twitch. "I can't. It's embarrassing."

She laughs as I lean over and nuzzle her neck. "Tell me, Chloe. I want to know everything I do to you."

"Well, that makes me tingle."

"Where?"

"Everywhere."

Her amused expression makes me smile as I raise my head. "Like here?"

I cup her breast, running my thumb across the hardened nipple.

"Uh huh." She raises her eyebrows.

Sliding my hand down over her stomach, I slip a finger into her pussy. "And what about here?"

"Oh, definitely there." Her eyes widen and her smile grows. "Oh, yes please."

I chuckle. "You like that?"

"I like it a lot." She raises her hand to run her fingers through my beard. "I like you."

"Then maybe you've got a little more time for me to show you how much I like you?"

She reaches up to stroke my cheek. "I'm sure I can squeeze you in."

I know I'll wake to an empty bed, but she's still warm beside me when I fall back asleep.

That's the last thing I remember.

FIFTEEN

CHLOE

I LIE there in his arms until I'm sure he's asleep.

Staying here would be the easiest thing in the world to do. The thought of being with him was both exhilarating and terrifying, but I conquered my fear and showed him how I felt.

All we need now is time.

My feelings are still confusing, but I know Hunter is who I want to be with.

I slide out of bed and open a drawer. A row of neatly folded shirts greets me, and I grab a button-down plaid shirt and slip it over my head. It's large and long on me, and covers everything for my journey back home.

After one last look at him, I make my way downstairs, press the button on the back door lock, and sneak out into the night, closing the door behind me.

I shiver, wrapping my arms around myself and take a deep breath of the cool air. I did it. I took the leap I was never sure I would take, and it was so worth it.

He wants more. And I think I do too, but that's another leap. I want to be decisive and push forward, but I owe it to myself to take my time and be sure. Once, I committed to spending my life with one person. Now, I'm starting again but still want to be able to commit to that. Whether it's to Hunter or someone else, I want a partner for a lifetime.

I hope it's Hunter; I want it to be.

Running through the backyard as the morning sun creeps into view feels scandalous. My bikini lies on the ground beside the lounger. I'm still not sure what possessed me to do what I did last night, but I managed to convey my message.

Reaching the inside of the house, I throw my bikini in the washing machine and head upstairs. My alarm's set for seven and it's six now, so there's still a little time for sleep. I'll go back to bed once I've taken the boys to school.

My bed's cold, and I regret that I left a warm bed for it. I'm not even sure I'll get any sleep because my heart's still racing at the thought of our night together.

I'll admit to mixed feelings because I never thought I'd ever be with anyone else, but for the first time in so long my heart is full. And I feel Hunter's presence even if he's still next door.

I close my eyes. In my head, I'm in Hunter's bed with him, his arms wrapped around my body as if to protect me. With him, I feel safe in a way I haven't felt for so long.

I can't stop smiling to myself at the thought of his hands on me. And of course, it's right as I'm drifting off that the alarm goes.

BRADEN AND XANDER are already in the kitchen when I make my way downstairs.

The sound of them scraping their cereal bowls clean fills the quiet kitchen as I put my morning coffee together.

The location of the coffee machine is still a mystery, but there are still boxes to unpack, and I've been a bit distracted lately.

I sit at the table with them.

"Are you okay, Mum?"

I blink and focus on Braden. "Uh, I'm fine. Just a little tired. I didn't sleep very well last night."

He shrugs. "I'm still getting used to this place too. I like it, though, and I'm glad we came here."

I smile. "I'm happy to hear that."

"Knowing Dad wanted us to live here makes a difference. I keep imagining what it would be like if he was here."

Reaching across the table, I place my hand on his. "I know I've said this before, but he'd be proud of you."

His brows drop. "Is that a new nightie? I've never seen that before."

I freeze. Will he recognise this as one of Hunter's shirts? I didn't even think about it before I rolled out of bed.

"Yeah. It's getting a little chilly at night."

He shoots me a quizzical look because he'll know I'm talking crap. But it's the first thing I think of and it'll have to do.

"Hey." Hunter's smiling face appears in the doorway.

"Hi." My cheeks heat up, and I can't help my shy reaction to him, as if he didn't just spend most of the night with his hands all over my body, leaving me with this wonderful ache that won't go away.

"Want a coffee, Hunter?" Braden's on his feet, heading to the kettle before Hunter even responds.

He nods. "That'd be great. I just thought I'd pop in to see if you and your brother wanted a ride to school. I've got to go to the office, and it's on my way ..."

"Mum?" Braden turns to look at me.

"Sure. I don't have a problem with that."

Last time I agreed to this, I was hung over and felt like death. Allowing my boys to ride in a car driven by anyone else but me still scares me, but I trust Hunter. He's done the school run before, and he'll take good care of my boys. My first instinct is to wrap them in cotton wool, but I have to learn to let go a little. This is as good a place to start as any and will help his relationship with them.

"I'll just make that coffee." Braden turns back to the kettle.

I shift my gaze to Hunter. His smile makes me suck in a breath, and I shoot one back before looking down at my own coffee.

He's the light at the end of the tunnel.

Can he be the same thing for my children?

IT'S the weirdest feeling when they're gone.

Last time Hunter brought my boys home, I was asleep. Now my nerves are eating at me as I watch the clock. All I want to do is go back to bed.

I pick up and put down my phone fifty times, worrying about them getting to school in one piece.

The door opens and sunlight floods the kitchen. Hunter fills the doorway, a big grin on his face. "I thought you should know the boys are safe at school."

I stand as he walks in and closes the door behind him.

"Is that my shirt?"

I look down and laugh. "I stole it."

"It looks good on you." The butterflies in my stomach take off as he draws closer. "But I think it'll look better *off* you."

My mouth falls open. "You are terrible."

"I've been thinking about you since I woke up this morning."

He closes the gap between us, pulling me to him and claiming my mouth with a crushing kiss that sears my soul.

There's zero doubt in my mind that Hunter loves me.

"Come here." He sits at the kitchen table and pulls me onto his lap. "What are your plans for the day?"

"I should be writing." I lean my head to the side as he nuzzles my neck. "But I have a feeling you have other plans."

"Actually, I thought I'd come over and sleep with you."

"Didn't we do that last night?" I laugh.

"I don't know about you, but I could do with some more actual sleep." The words vibrate against my neck and I sigh.

"Me too. Can we go to your place?"

He pulls me around so I'm sitting sideways on his lap and scans my expression. "You don't want to stay here?"

I bite my bottom lip. "If it was just sleeping, I would, but ... I don't think it will be, and that wouldn't feel right."

"Why not?" He frowns.

I should just come out and say it. Relationships aren't built on holding back.

"I still have the bed that Scott and I shared."

Understanding crosses his face. "Then we'll go to my place. I replaced my bed after ... everything."

"Hunter Emerson, are you saying I'm the first woman you've had in that bed?"

"First and only. I don't want anyone else."

I run my fingers through his hair. "Let's go to your house, then. I'll grab some clothes so I can get changed there."

He nods. "That sounds like a plan."

After one last lingering kiss, he lets me go, and I run upstairs and throw together a few things to wear. I grab my phone and keys on the way out and lock up the house.

This feels naughty.

It's like I'm breaking every rule, but there are no rules.

I tug off the shirt before climbing into bed with him. It's different in the daylight. He's gentle. And I don't ask him for anything else because I think it's what we both need.

Now I know what falling in love is like. It's the butterflies that persist even when I'm the one in his bed and in his arms. It's those giddy moments when his lips graze my neck and his hands roam my body.

And if this is falling, I don't ever want to land.

"Chloe," he whispers, his thrusts long and slow. My spine tingles when he says my name in that deep voice of his.

I close my eyes as he kisses me, his lips caressing mine.

It's so easy to lose myself to him.

And afterward, he holds me in his arms and says nothing. The moment washes over us peacefully as if we've been doing this every day for years.

He feels like home.

"Last night was one of the best nights of my life." I raise my gaze to meet his.

Hunter's dark eyes give away nothing, but his lips curl into a smile. "Last night was *the* best night of my life," he replies.

I swallow hard and press my palm to his chest. "That's a pretty big statement."

"It was amazing. You're amazing." He places his hand on my palm. "I don't want it to be a one-off."

I smile. "Neither do I."

"Then, let's get some sleep before the boys need picking up."

I roll to my side and he spoons me from behind, just as he did in my bed. But now it means more.

I've been alone for four years.

It's a hard state to get used to when you've been with someone your whole life, but it's even harder to process that I'm not alone anymore.

I have Hunter.

SIXTEEN
HUNTER

IT'S BEEN TWO WEEKS. Chloe's slept over most nights, though the weekends are a bit more difficult as the boys are up later.

And I've been terrible as far as the romance goes.

She arrives, and we end up in bed, which is amazing but not all I want with her.

But that's about to change.

The day seems to take an eternity, but thankfully, I'm busy with work.

"How's Gary doing?" I ask Liz.

"He's good. The counselling seems to be helping. You haven't had any late night calls, have you?"

I shake my head. She's much better at the HR side of the business than I am. I need to just hand it all over to her.

"What I do need to do is work out whether to send him to get his First Aid certificate renewed." She chews on her bottom lip. "Or do we wait a bit longer?"

"If it's due, send him. You know I like the guys to be up to date with their training."

She nods. "I was just thinking if he does end up leaving, or we have to terminate him, there's the cost to be recovered."

I blow out a breath. "Let's just do it and swallow the cost if we have to. He's making the effort we asked him to, even if it's a bit late."

"You're a good man, Hunter."

I tap her desk with my pen. "And you are a good woman. I think we need to take another look at your job because you're doing things I never anticipated, and you should be rewarded for that."

Liz grins. "Whoever this new lady is must be doing you the world of good."

"Why do you say that?"

"You already pay me a generous wage, Hunter."

I shake my head. "With everything you've done lately, I don't think it's enough."

"Well, let's deal with it tomorrow because I'm sick of today and ready to go home." She smiles.

"Sounds good." I grab my jacket. "I'll probably be in the office at some point in the morning. We can discuss it then."

Liz slings her handbag over her shoulder. "We can."

She switches off the light and locks the door behind us. I wave and walk to my car, my steps lighter than usual.

Chloe's waiting.

Even if we're keeping us a secret for now.

CHLOE: *I'll be over about ten if that's okay.*

Me: *I'm ready when you are.*

Chloe: *I can't wait to see you.*

I have plans for her tonight. I'm sure we'll end up in bed, but I can't stop thinking about what Chloe's brother said.

She needs more.

She deserves more.

So I prepare and wait.

A little after ten, she appears in the doorway, breathless, her eyes filled with need.

"I've been thinking about this all day."

I pull her into my arms. "Me too."

"Take me to bed," she whispers.

"I feel like I've been waiting years for you to say that to me."

Her lips twitch. "Less talk, more action, Emerson."

"Sorry for the delay."

She squeals as I bend and throw her over my shoulder. Instead of heading upstairs, I carry her into the living room and deposit her on the couch. Her eyes widen at the candle-lit room and the big bowl of popcorn on the coffee table.

"What's going on?"

I lean over and give her a tender kiss. "I thought we could cuddle on the couch and watch a movie. It's your choice. The last Avengers movie, or The Notebook."

Her face lights up in a dazzling smile. "I love that idea. Which one do you want to watch?"

"I haven't seen either, and I'm happy either way. I just want to spend some time with you."

She bites her bottom lip. "Well, I'm way more partial to action movies."

"I remember."

For a moment, her expression blanks, but then she blinks rapidly, and waves of emotion seem to overtake her. "You remember?"

"I fell in love with you when we were fifteen years old. I remember."

Chloe's eyes light up. "Hunter." She reaches over, caressing my cheek with her palm. "I don't know what to say."

"You don't have to say anything. I know you loved him, and I'm not trying to replace him." I draw a deep breath. "All I want is a part of your heart just for me."

Her eyes mist over. "You've got it. A rather large chunk of it if I'm honest."

I smile. "Really?"

"Hunter, I'm not just here for sex. Although, it is amazing." She pauses, sucking on her bottom lip like she's trying to work out what else to say. "I miss having a companion. I miss having someone to share those special moments with."

"I'll give you all the special moments." I adore this woman. She's everything I ever thought she'd be. I want her and only her.

She smiles before leaning closer and pressing her forehead to mine. All I can smell is her lip gloss.

"Let's watch this movie," I say.

Chloe pulls back a little, and my heart leaps just looking at her. She gazes at me with so much love in her expression, and I'm right along with her. Our past and attraction to each other is one thing, but this friendship we've formed has turned into something else. And for the first time in so long, I have hope in my life.

I think I've given her the same.

She reaches for the popcorn.

"Let's get this movie started. It's long," I say.

"There's a good chance I'll fall asleep."

I laugh. "If that happens, it happens."

Chloe smiles, tosses some popcorn into her mouth, then snuggles back into my chest.

Life is perfect.

IT'S one in the morning when we finally get to bed.

We lie in the quiet, and I close my eyes and listen to the soft sound of her breathing. It's comforting, but knowing she'll leave in the night makes my heart ache.

"What are you thinking about?" I ask.

Chloe plants a kiss on my chest. "How good this all feels. I know you have my back. It's been a while."

I run my hand up her arm. "That's because I want to be with you. Not just in the night, but for always."

"I know." She sighs. "It's just ... you make me feel safe even when we're not together. And I like that feeling so much. It's made me realise just how alone I really have been up until now. You're making a difference."

She tilts her head back, and I scan her face before kissing her softly.

"I want to be the man who makes that difference. And, one day, the man who comes home to you at night, and wakes up with you in the morning."

Her expression softens. "I want all that too. But before we get there, I want romance and everything that comes with falling in love." Chloe runs her fingers over my abs. "Maybe you should ask me out."

"Is that allowed?"

She shrugs. "It's a good way to ease the kids into it while I continue to sneak over here to fulfil our mutual need for each other."

I chuckle. "Is that what you call it?"

She traces circles on my chest. "I know it's what I feel. And it's more than just sex. I really enjoyed tonight."

"Me too. Next time, I'll take you to the movies."

Chloe grins. "I haven't been to a cinema in ... I don't know how long."

"Then, we'll fix that. Maybe we can find something the boys will like too." I ponder for a moment. "But then I don't think they'll like it much if we're making out in the back row."

She laughs. "Taking them might not be such a good idea. Besides, they rarely agree on anything, let alone which movie to watch."

"And there's our other problem." I kiss her nose. "Hey, how about I go and make us a hot chocolate, and we can get a few hours sleep before you head home."

"That sounds wonderful."

"I'll set the alarm so you don't oversleep."

I pull myself away, and as I slip out of bed, her hand closes around my wrist.

"Thank you."

Smiling I bend and kiss her knuckles. "I'd do anything for you, Chloe Cooper. Just remember that."

I tug on my boxers and make my way to the kitchen, whistling the whole way.

Chloe talks about healing her heart, but she's doing a good job of healing mine too.

SEVENTEEN
CHLOE

"GOT YOU."

After dropping the boys at school, I came home determined to find the box with the coffee machine in it. For some reason, it ended up at the bottom of Braden's wardrobe, but I finally get my hands on it and kiss the box.

Once it's plugged in, I'll head to the supermarket and buy some real coffee.

"I've missed you so much, my baby." I croon as I carry it down the stairs.

This is such a big a part of my writing routine, and I've been lost without it. The coffee machine alone will make this house feel more like home. Although, it's getting old in the tooth. I bought it with the first decent royalties I made, and Scott used to laugh and call it our third child—I loved it so much.

"I swear you love that machine more than me." He laughs as I plug it in. "Look at you. You're focusing so hard on it, your tongue's sticking out."

I turn and poke my tongue at him.

"Have I told you how proud I am of you?" Scott wraps his arms

around my waist from behind. "I know you went a long time without being able to fulfil your dreams. And now look."

I press the on button, and the machine lights up. "My dream to own a coffee machine?"

"Chloe." He laughs and turns me around. "You gave up a lot for our boys and me when I was at uni. It's your turn, babe."

I place the machine on the bench and take a deep breath. There are so many ways I could make my life easier. I still have to add the beans and froth the milk manually while there are newer machines that do it all for you.

But this machine has so much meaning.

And I need to celebrate finding it by having a real coffee.

Time to go to the supermarket.

I BUY a selection of coffee because I can't make up my mind and, over time, I'll drink it all anyway.

As I browse the shelves, out of the corner of my eye I spot someone waving.

"Chloe? Chloe Baxter?"

I look up. Piper Edwards. At least that's how I knew her at school.

She married Hunter.

My Hunter.

"Piper."

She smiles. "You remember."

"It's Chloe Cooper now."

Piper nods. "Of course it is. How are you? How's Scott?"

I swallow hard. A short time ago that question would have still broken me, but a lot's changed since I got back to town.

"Scott died about four years ago. I just moved back to town with my kids."

Her expression straightens. "I'm so sorry to hear that."

"We're doing okay. It's good to see you."

"Good to see you too." She seems to hesitate. "Have you seen Hunter?"

I draw in a deep breath. "We're neighbours."

Her nose twitches. "Really?"

I smile. "I bought the house next door. Didn't realise until after we'd moved in."

It's so hard to know what she's thinking. I don't remember much about her from school other than her antagonistic relationship with Hunter, which apparently wasn't all it seemed. And I'm not envious of her. She had her chance, and for whatever reason she chose the path she did.

And now the man she didn't want is mine.

"He'll like that," she snaps, as if I planned to move next door to him.

"He does. So do I." There's no way I'm going to let her bother me. We were never close back then, and there's no reason for us to be now. "It's been good to renew old friendships. I had dinner with Meredith and Darren Carmichael a while ago too."

She screws up her face. "I haven't seen them in a long time. Meredith got all huffy with me when Hunter and I split."

I clamp my lips together. Piper was always a prickly person. It's what surprised me the most about her being with Hunter in the first place. They were nothing alike.

"She's very loyal to him."

Piper looks me up and down. "Yeah, she is."

I hold up my palms. "Look. I don't know the finer details of what happened between you and Hunter, but I'd prefer it if there wasn't any animosity between us."

She's silent for a moment. "Sure."

"Anyway, I've got to get these groceries and get back home to do some work. Have a good day, Piper."

She doesn't even respond as I walk away.

That's that, then.

BACK IN THE CAR, with my coffee and a big bag of donuts, I take a deep breath.

I don't have anything against Piper. And she really shouldn't have anything against me. I didn't hurt her. I didn't steal her husband. She doesn't even know about Hunter and me.

I'm not sure what put a stick up her arse where I'm concerned, but I can't do anything about it. I don't even want to.

My phone buzzes, and I pull it out of my bag.

Meredith's name pops up on the screen and I smile.

"Hi, Meredith."

"Chloe. Have I caught you at a good time?"

I laugh. "I'm just about to drive home with my groceries. Timing is perfect."

"I wondered if you wanted to go somewhere for a coffee."

"Yes. I'd love to. That sounds great and just what I need right now."

"There's a place ..." She pauses. "Are you okay?"

"I'll tell you when I see you."

"There's a place not far from the school in case you have to pick up your boys. I'll text you the details. How about we make it one-thirty, and that'll give us an hour before I have to go and get my kids."

Sighing after the call is disconnected, I slip my phone into my bag and head home to drop off the groceries. Hunter's car isn't in his driveway, but I'll see him later to update him about my morning. It's probably a good thing in some ways because I'd only be tempted to go over early and not get any work done.

The time is just after eleven, and I have work to do.

FINDING THE CAFE IS EASY. Meredith was right, it's just down the road from the boys' school.

She smiles as I walk in the door.

After ordering coffee, I take a seat opposite her.

"It's so good to see you, Chloe. You're looking well."

I smile. "You too. How's the family?"

Her face lights up. "Good. How about yours?"

"We're good too. The boys are settled in to school and making friends. Xander made the first fifteen and starts training soon."

"Flat white?" A waitress places my coffee in front of me.

"Thank you." I take a sip. "Oh, that's good coffee."

"I love this place," Meredith says. "My kids' school isn't far from here either, and the food's good too."

"I just really need coffee today. It's been a long one." I take another sip. "I ran into Piper at the supermarket this morning."

She rolls her eyes. "Ugh. How did *that* go?"

Her response makes me laugh. "She didn't seem too happy to see me. Which, to be honest, is weird because we never had that much to do with each other."

"She really fucked Hunter over. I'd be happy if I never saw her again."

I suck on my bottom lip. "What did she do? I mean, he told me she cheated, but ..."

"He had to buy her out of everything. Which is fine because she was entitled to it. But she broke him. I always had this weird feeling about her, like he was way more into her than she was into him. So when he caught her in his own bed with some other guy, he was devastated."

Tears prick my eyes. I can't even imagine what that must have been like for him. Finding Scott like that would have killed me.

"And then he self-destructed. Seemed to think it was his mission to bang anything that moved. He stopped coming around to our place because we didn't want the kids to meet woman number five only for woman number six to be with him a week later."

I swallow hard.

"Anyway, it was like that for about six months, and once she was paid out of the house and the business, he got his shit together. He became a bit more like the Hunter I remembered because I didn't recognise him for a while." "And now," she continues. "You and Hunter." Her raised eyebrows give away what she's thinking. It's almost a relief after the unreadable Piper.

"Yes."

"Yes, you two are together, or ..."

I bite my bottom lip. Meredith was never anyone I confided in, but she's a friend.

"We are, but we're keeping it low key."

She grins. "I knew it. Was it before you came to dinner?"

I shake my head. "After. But your dinner was an eye opener. I never thought of him in that way before."

Meredith fans herself with her hand. "*I* nearly jumped him that night. That was so hot. I almost called you the next day, but I thought I'd better leave that alone for a while."

I nod. "It took a little while. And I haven't told the boys yet. So, I think it'll be a while before we announce anything to the world." I take a sip of my coffee. "Besides, I'm enjoying it just being us."

"I won't tell Darren. He thought something was going on the other night, but he hasn't mentioned it again." She leans forward. "It's the most perceptive he's been for a while. Usually, you two could have sex on our dining table and Darren would probably still miss it."

Laughing, I shake my head. "I'm sure he's not that bad."

"No. But he's still good at missing the obvious. I'll let him work it out, unless Hunter tells him."

"Thank you."

She shrugs. "You're welcome. And you haven't been back long, so I'm guessing you haven't made a lot of new friends. I'm not going to screw you over. I'm glad you're back."

"Me too." I smile. "Me too."

"I think you might just be what each other needs. He's been alone the past three years, Chloe. As far as I know there's not been anyone else. And he did always have the biggest crush on you."

I sigh. "I had no idea."

"It's all water under the bridge now, but I think you'll be good together."

I pick up my cup and smile behind it.

I think Meredith is right.

EIGHTEEN

HUNTER

"I RAN into Piper at the supermarket this morning."

I grit my teeth. Things didn't end well between Piper and me. And she always resented I crushed on Chloe in high school and not her.

"What happened to you two?"

I thought she might ask at some point, and I'm not sure how well she'll take the whole story. But she's lying in my arms in my bed, and if I don't tell her the whole story, I'm sure Piper will relish the opportunity if she thinks it'll hurt me.

"Your house. The last couple who lived there."

Chloe nods.

"We got to know them. The fence broke and we had already established a friendship with them, so didn't bother getting it fixed at that point."

Chloe's brows knit. "I know that much."

"Anyway, we were in and out of each other's houses. Two childless couples with free evenings." I raise my arms to rest behind my head. "It turned out our new neighbours were swingers." I open my eye and take in the look on Chloe's face.

Her eyes widen. "Really?"

"Yes, and after a few drinks one night, they suggested we swap partners for the evening. I'm not even sure where the idea came from. I wasn't keen on the idea, but Piper thought it was a huge turn on, and I would have done anything for her at that stage."

Chloe draws in a big breath.

"Anyway, I woke up in the morning wishing we hadn't done it. Piper wanted to do it again. We argued. She kept sleeping with *him*. I didn't know until I caught them in my own bed."

"Oh, Hunter." Chloe's face is full of sympathy. "I'm so sorry."

"So, then I went a bit stir crazy after she left. Slept with a lot of women, and have a lot of regrets." I sigh. "And then I woke up one morning and wondered what the hell I was doing. Piper was gone, and I had the rest of my life to live." I lick my lips and press a kiss to her forehead. "And then three years later, you show up. And you bring that sunshine back that you always did. I'm not sure where this is going, Chloe, but I can't tell you how good it is to have you in my life again."

She places her warm palm on my chest. "It might be a surprise to you, but you're only the second man I've ever slept with."

I chuckle. "I kind of worked that out."

"Maybe I should have done my own sleeping around town to make myself feel better, but I don't think I could do it. I need the emotional connection."

I scan her expression. "We have that."

"You're the only one I have that with. One of Scott's co-workers used to visit me in Auckland. We were kind of friends before he propositioned me, and it was tempting because sex would have been nice, but it didn't feel right."

Her blue eyes are full of affection as she gazes at me.

"But it feels right with me?"

She nods. "It's not just sex with you. This is deeper. And it feels right."

"Besides, I'm really good at it."

For a second, she takes me seriously before her face crumbles and her body shakes with laughter. "Yes, Hunter. You're very good at it."

"Sit on my face and tell me how good I am."

Her eyebrows rise. "I'm not sure ..."

"Live a little, Chloe. I'll show you how good sex can be."

Amusement fills her expression. "Hunter, I don't know ..."

"Trust me."

"I've never done anything like that before. I've always been pretty vanilla."

I lean forward a bit. "I'm not spanking you. I just want to eat your pussy."

Her cheeks pink up. I don't think she's ever been spoken to this way. She squirms beside me, and I don't need to ask her if she's thinking about it. I'm used to vocalising what I want.

"Just think about it, Chloe ... My beard tickling your thighs."

She lets out a tiny gasp and inches closer to me, her body telling me a story she doesn't need to verbalise.

"You're so not used to this and it's the most adorable thing ever."

She laughs and gives me a gentle slap. "No, I'm not used to it. No one ever just said these things to me."

"Is this the part where I tell you just how much I love the way your body moulds to mine when we're in bed together? It's like we're two halves of a whole that finally reached the point in their lives where they're the perfect fit."

Chloe traces her finger over my abdominal muscles. "That didn't get as dirty as I thought it was going to be."

I kiss her ear. "Then maybe I should also tell you how good it feels to be inside you, and how your pussy grips me tight."

"Hunter." Her tone tells me she's amused, but not offended.

"Just telling it like it is." I shrug.

She sucks on her bottom lip. "So, you really want me to ..."

"I want you to be as free as you were that first night we were together. When you wanted me to fuck you so hard that you'd feel it the next day."

Her lips curl into a smile. "And I did."

"You've been trapped, Chlo. These past four years, this beautiful woman I know who is so full of love has had to deal with all the shitty things life has thrown at her. And I bet not once did you ever ask for anything for yourself."

Her eyes search mine, and I know I've hit a sore spot. But she slowly nods again.

"Let me be the man to give it all to you. Maybe we weren't destined for each other originally, but I'd like to think fate brought us together for a reason. And I'm willing to sacrifice my body." I smile.

Chloe laughs. "I love being with you."

I run my fingers through her hair. "You coming back to town is the best thing to ever happen to me."

"It makes me really happy to hear that." She smacks her lips together and looks up at the headboard. "Okay, I'll ride your face." She giggles.

"Come on over." I grin.

She rises up on her knees and I let out a low whistle.

Chloe wags her index finger at me. "Stop it, or you'll miss out."

I laugh as she straddles my head.

"I can't believe I'm doing it."

I grip her thighs. "I fucking love that you're doing it."

The headboard moves behind me as she takes hold of it.

"Oh my God, Hunter. I'm too old for this."

"You're looking good from where I am."

She lowers herself a little, and I pull her the rest of the way. Chloe squeals with laughter.

"That's my girl."

I feast on her as she squirms above me. Sliding my hands up her torso, I cup her breasts.

She gasps. "Hunter."

I love this. I love that I'm giving her experiences she's clearly never had before. Then again, our first night taught me how unpredictable she is. And she's right; my first instinct was to treat her like china, but now I know she likes it hard and rough, and from the way she's reacting, she likes this too.

There's so much for us to explore together.

If she'd decided not to do this, I wouldn't have a problem with it. But that she's chosen to move out of her comfort zone means a lot, and I'm going to make her come so hard her legs turn to jelly.

I ignore my instinct to treat her gently and suck on her clit.

She lets out a moan that makes my cock twitch. And then she whimpers when I run my tongue up her slit.

"Hunter."

My name on her lips urges me on as I tease her, circling her clit with my tongue before sucking on it again.

Her body shakes, and the headboard slams the wall. I grin, losing myself in her scent and taste. She's everything I ever wanted.

Chloe's perfect.

Again and again, she grinds against me, and I don't even know if she knows it but I love it. She's so into it, and she comes for the second time right as I lap at her clit again.

I squeeze her thighs, and slide out from underneath her. She turns, letting go of the headboard and throws herself at me as I sit up.

Her mouth is on mine in an instant, and I kiss her back as hard as she's kissing me. My beard's covered in her, and she's all I can smell.

I roll her until she's lying on her back but keep kissing her, not ready to break the contact.

Letting her up for air, I take in the sight of her.

"I ..." Her cheeks are flushed, and her eyes are so alive. "That was crazy."

I chuckle, and she drops her gaze.

"Hey. I'm glad you liked it."

"You must think I'm so naive, but I'd never done that before."

I shake my head. "No. I think you're a woman who became a mother really early, and your whole life was consumed by it. I'm not going for a comparison."

She nods. "You're right. I wouldn't give them up for anything, but having the twins changed us. Gone were the days of sex in the back seat of the car."

"Well, you know I'm up for it if you are."

Chloe laughs. "I'm not sure. You're so big."

"I'll take that as a compliment."

She slaps my chest again. "I'd rather be in this warm, comfortable bed with you."

"I'm fine with that. And I'll add sitting on my face to my list of things you enjoy."

She laughs, burying her face in my side.

"You can add anything you want to that list, you know."

Her head pops up. "Anything?"

My eyebrows rise. "Sure. Although, with that tone, I'm really wondering what's coming next."

"I just want you to hold me, Hunter. You make me feel safer than I have in a long time."

"It's because I'm like a giant teddy bear, right?"

Chloe laughs again. "Maybe. And maybe it's because I can trust you completely. With my body and my heart."

I wrap my arms around her and close my eyes. She has so much affection to give, and not a huge amount of worldly experience. I can return that affection and give her so much more.

"Hunter," she whispers.

"Yes?"

"Sleeping with your neighbour isn't always a bad idea."

Her body trembles again with laughter, and all I can do is shake my head in amusement.

"You're the only neighbour I should have ever slept with." I open my eyes and meet her gaze. Her smile gets me every time, and I smile back at her.

"Now we've settled that, let's get some sleep." She yawns.

"The alarm's set."

"I sleep better when I'm with you."

That's the last thing she says before her breath on my chest slows.

I'm in love with Chloe all over again. It's impossible not to be. Only this time, we can be together—all I have to do is be patient and give her time. Which isn't easy when you're not a patient man.

Maybe that's something Chloe can help teach me.

NINETEEN
HUNTER

I TAP my fingers on my desk as the website takes forever to load.

"Hey, Liz," I call.

"Yes?"

"Is the internet usually this slow?"

She laughs, appearing in the doorway. "How have you not noticed?"

"I've been using it at home and it's been fast. I guess I should upgrade this."

"Yes, please."

"You know you have the authority to make those kinds of changes, don't you?"

She crosses her arms and leans against the doorway. "Now you tell me."

"When I'm not here, you're the boss. Hell, you're really the one running the place."

Liz grins. "You're hopeless. Why are you even here?"

"I just wanted to check some contracts."

She walks in and around my desk before taking a look at my screen. "Do those clients need flowers sent?"

"Uh ...."

Cocking her head, she seems to be suppressing a smile. "These aren't for clients, are they?"

"The site's so slow. Which ones do you like?"

She sighs. "What ones did you used to send?"

"I'm not sending Chloe the same flowers I used to send Piper. That's just wrong."

She smiles smugly. "So Chloe's her name?"

I laugh. "Yes, and I want to impress her. I mean, I'm not sure I need to, but ..."

"Send her red roses. Those always work."

"Aren't they a bit over the top?"

She grips my shoulder. "You really like this woman, don't you? Just do it. She'll love it. I promise."

"Okay."

The site's still slow, but I click through, ordering a dozen red roses for delivery. I can't help but feel that it's corny, but as long as Chloe loves it, I'll be happy. And they can be delivered before the boys get home so she can tell them whatever she wants.

It's tiring keeping this to us, but everything's going so well, I don't want to rock the boat.

I love her.

THE KITCHEN DOOR opens right as I'm pouring a drink.

"I got the flowers." Her eyes shine with happiness. "They were lovely. Thank you."

"Didn't cause any issues with the boys?"

She shakes her head. "I don't even know if they noticed them. They're in a vase in the middle of the kitchen table and they both walked past without saying a thing."

I chuckle. "I was worried there might be trouble."

"No trouble. I think they just assumed I bought them for myself. I've bought flowers before."

I grasp her hands. "I'm glad you liked them. Now, I don't know about you, but I'm tired tonight. I just want to go to bed and hold you."

Chloe smiles. "I'd really like that. All these late nights are getting to me."

"Me too. I'm way too old for this." I lead her up the stairs to my bedroom.

"We're the same age. That makes me too old too."

When we're inside the room, I pull her into my arms. "I want to grow old with you, Chloe."

She says nothing but raises her hand to stroke my beard. It's her move, and I love it. I'll never shave it off if she likes it that much.

Chloe presses her hands to my chest, never dropping her gaze before undoing the buttons on my shirt. Her hands are warm and soft, and her touch makes me hard as a rock.

I don't think we'll be going straight to sleep.

She lays her palms flat on my pecs.

"I love you touching me," I say.

"Feeling's mutual." Her eyes are so expressive. We haven't said I love you, but I can see it, feel it.

I reach for the bottom of her T-shirt, and for a moment her hands lose contact as I raise it over her head. She smiles, reaches for the clasps of her bra, and undoes it before dropping it to the ground.

"You still have my shirt at home?" I ask.

"You're not getting it back."

She laughs as she slips off her jeans and climbs into my bed. I drop my pants to the floor and get in beside her.

She's only in my arms for about thirty seconds before she cups my cock.

"We were going to sleep."

"Doesn't have to take long." Her flirty smile undoes me.

"You're not doing my ego any good with that comment."

Chloe laughs. "You know what I mean."

I slide my hand up her leg, and her breath hitches. Nuzzling her neck, I slip my hand into her panties.

There's still a part of me that can't quite believe this is real. Making Chloe come has to be my favourite thing to do.

When we're both ready, I slide into her, and close my eyes as her heat closes around me. I'm so in love with Chloe. I meant what I said before: this is the woman I want to grow old with.

Her lips taste of her coconut gloss. It's so familiar now I crave it when I'm not around her.

Moving slowly, I keep kissing her. It's so easy to get lost in her when she's all I want.

I drop my lips to her neck.

"Scott," she whispers.

It's just one word, but it's not a name I want to hear. Not now.

Her eyes fly open. "Hunter. I'm so sorry. I didn't mean ..."

I pull out of her, roll over onto my back, and stare at the ceiling as she turns toward me.

This is so hard.

"Hunter. Please."

"Who is it that you see when we're together, Chloe?"

"You."

I turn my head to look at her. "Are you sure?"

"Yes. I don't know why I said it. It's you I want."

I sit up, dropping my legs to the floor. "The thing is, I'm in love with you. I loved you when we were kids, and I love you now. And I only love you. I'm not angry that you're still in love with Scott. It's only natural. But I need to know you love me for me."

Chloe shuffles over the bed and places her hand on my back. "Hunter."

I turn my head. "I love you, Chloe, but I need to hear it from you and know it's true."

Her eyes fill with tears.

"You can't say it yet."

She blinks. "I'm not sure what I feel. It's so big and overwhelming, and all I want to do is be with you. But I can't remember falling in love the first time around, so I'm trying to work out these emotions."

"I think maybe you should go home."

Chloe blinks a bunch of times and nods. I'm glad she's not fighting me on this because I need some time to clear my mind. I know how I feel about her, but will she ever feel the same way about me?

What if we've been so swept up in this new-found lust for each other that it's all this can ever be for her?

The weight on the bed shifts, and I look up to see the woman I'm so madly in love with walking naked out the door. The bathroom light floods the hallway before fading as she shuts herself in.

Maybe I'm being selfish. Maybe I should understand there'll be times that she thinks of Scott. But that doesn't make her calling out his name while we were making love any easier.

I really thought she was mine.

The bathroom door creaks.

Her hands cup my face and pull it up so I'm looking into her eyes. She doesn't say a word but leans over and gives me a soft, lingering kiss on the lips.

"Please don't be angry," she whispers.

"I'm not angry. How can I be? I feel selfish for wanting it, but I need to know you're mine."

Chloe presses her forehead to mine. "I am yours. I've not been anyone else's for a long time. I screwed up, and I'll own that. But I don't want to lose you in the process."

I close my eyes. "There's no way you *can lose* me. I belong to you, Chloe. No matter how long it takes. But I won't be your friend with benefits. I want it all."

She pulls back, and for a woman whose eyes are so expressive, all I see is confusion. Maybe her slip-up is a good thing. It's making us both examine whatever this is between us more closely.

I thought what we had was enough, but I do want it all.

I want to be her husband. I want to be Braden and Xander's stepfather. I want to give her more children like she always wanted. She's the one I want to have my children with. But I can't be all of that if she's not ready for me to be.

She bends and picks up my shirt from the floor before slipping it over her head. "I'm taking this."

I stifle a laugh. "I love you, Chloe."

"I know you do. And you're right. It's not fair to you that I can't say it back yet. But I don't want anyone else either, so you're stuck with me when I finish getting myself together."

I grab hold of her hand. "I'm not trying to push you. Take your time."

She nods. "I know. If we're going to be together, you deserve all of me, and that includes having a relationship out in the open."

"What if this is all it is?" It hurts so damn much to ask the question, but I have to. Are we in the shadows because this is the limit of our relationship?

"It can't be."

And with that, she slips into the night and I'm left alone with my thoughts.

He'll always be there and a reminder of what she used to have.

How do I compete with that?

TWENTY
CHLOE

TONIGHT WAS AWFUL.

I hurt Hunter, and the pain in his expression will be with me for a very long time. I'm not even sure how, but the word just spilled out at the wrong time, and now I have to work out what I want.

Who am I?

It was so easy falling into something with Hunter, and he's the one I want to be with. But I think I need to work myself out first.

This isn't the first time I've asked myself that question, but I did get swept away by this overwhelming attraction to Hunter and everything that went with it. I have no regrets about anything that happened between us. And I need to find a way back to that.

He's whom I want my future to be with.

I need to let my heart take that final step, but if I'm honest, I'm holding back.

Sighing, I slip into my cold bed and stare at the ceiling. I came home to bring my children back to the birthplace of their parents, to let them get to know their family here, and to bring my husband to his final resting place. And while the twins have settled into life here and made friends, I've not fulfilled my final promise to myself about Scott.

His ashes sit inside a small wooden box in the living room. He travelled in the car with us to our new home, but he's not been laid to rest yet.

"Mum?" I'm so tired I'm not even sure which of my sons appear at the door. As he draws closer, I realise it's Xander. "Where have you been?"

"I went out for a walk."

He slides into bed beside me. "At this time of night? It's not safe."

"I've just got a lot to think about right now."

I lean over and peck him on the forehead. He screws up his nose because he's told me before he's too old for that.

"I miss Dad."

Of all the nights to come to me with this ...

"I do too."

"And I like Hunter. Maybe you should invite him over more often."

Tears prick my eyes. "Are you saying that because you know he's my friend, or ..."

"I'm saying it because I think he likes you. And he's pretty good to Braden and me. Maybe then you wouldn't have to buy yourself flowers."

Despite it all, I laugh while tears pour down my cheeks, and he just looks at me with confusion all over his face.

"I know it's hard, Mum. Dad would have approved, I think."

"I think he would have too,' I whisper.

He rolls over, turning his back to me.

"Goodnight, Mum."

And for once, Braden doesn't join us, and I roll the other way. But sleep isn't coming any time soon.

There's still so much to work out.

SLEEP IS ALMOST NON-EXISTENT.

But in the quiet, once the boys are at school, I make my way to my bedroom and take a look at the bed.

Maybe this is where I start.

It didn't feel right to have Hunter over here while I still sleep in the bed Scott and I shared. If we are going to have a relationship, it has to be open and honest. I'll take that on board. In an effort to protect the boys, I think I took it a bit too far.

They both like Hunter; that much has been made crystal clear. And while I might not yet be ready to say I love you, he's stolen so much of my heart.

I just need to be Chloe for a little while.

After lunch, I'll go shopping for a new bed.

The morning drags, but it's productive even with distractions, and I'm champing at the bit to get out.

It's not a long drive to Bedpost, and I take a deep breath as I climb out of the car and look at the beds on display in the window.

I have to stop myself from thinking about what anyone else wants. *This is for me.*

Walking into the store, I head toward the biggest bed I can see and drag my fingers along the base of the mattress.

"Can I help you with anything?"

A young woman approaches with a cautious smile on her face.

"I'm looking for a new bed."

My stomach wavers just thinking about it.

Her smile widens. "You're in the right place. Was there anything in particular you were after?"

I let out a sigh. "I'm not sure where to start. I want a king size. Or even a super king. But I'm open to suggestions."

She pats the bed. "This is definitely an option, although it really depends on your budget and the bed type."

"I'm more concerned about finding the right bed than the budget." I look around. "Within reason. I'm making a fresh start, and I want something that's right for me."

"Take a seat and try out the mattress for yourself."

I sit down and bounce. "Do you have something a bit softer? This one's a bit stiff."

"Sure. Come this way."

I'm sure there's a spring in my step as we move to the next bed, and then the next. I sit on each one feeling a little like Goldilocks, never quite happy until I find the perfect fit.

And the second I sink into it, I know. "This I really like." Stretching out, I kick off my shoes and lie back. "Oh, yes. This is the one."

"We have this one in stock so just need to organise delivery."

"As soon as possible. Will they help me move the old bed to another room?"

She smiles. "I'm sure we can sort something out."

"Thank you."

"Do you need linen?" she asks.

I blow out a breath. If I'm going to make a fresh start, I should go the whole hog.

"Yes, I do."

"We've got a full range if you'd like to step this way ..."

I take a deep breath as I leave the store, laden with bags.

None of this is easy, but I can't play both sides. If I'm going to move on with my life, this is something that needs to happen regardless.

I'm nervous about all of this but excited to be doing something new.

I drop all the bags in the boot of the car and check the time. It's getting close to three, so I need to head toward the school and pick up the boys. I'm not sure what they'll think of all of this. Our bed was a big part of our past. It was common when the boys were little that they'd crawl in between Scott and me for cuddles in the morning.

It's not easy to say goodbye. But nothing's been easy for the past four years.

Pulling up outside the school, I wait for the bell to ring. Part of me wants to race home, strip and move the bed already, but there's no point doing that until the new one gets delivered in a few days.

Children pour out of the gates as the time hits three, and mine just about stumble over each other racing to the car.

I shake my head. Some things never change.

But this time, there's another boy with them.

"Shotgun," Braden yells.

Xander shrugs, which in itself isn't like him. He doesn't usually surrender so easily.

"Mum, this is Lincoln. He plays rugby with me. Can he get a lift with us?" Xander asks.

"Where does he live?"

"It's on the way home. He'll show you."

I nod. "Sure thing."

As I pull out and into traffic, I smile. Xander hasn't had close friends in a long time. I know it's a just a ride home, but him wanting to help out this kid speaks volumes.

Maybe everything really is falling into place.

Halfway back to our place, Xander points to a road on the left. "Just down here. What number is it?"

"Fourteen. It's about five houses down on the left."

"Roger that." I indicate and take the turn into the street.

After four houses, I slow to a crawl as Lincoln points out the house. It's an older place with cream weatherboards, and shuttered windows. There's no fence, but a large, well maintained front lawn. It's very pretty.

"Thanks, Mrs Cooper." Lincoln says.

"You're welcome, hon. If you ever need a lift home in future, you're always welcome."

He climbs out of the back seat with his bag, and leans over to speak to Xander. "See you tomorrow."

Xander chinlifts, and Lincoln does the same in response.

"Wait a moment." A woman's voice comes from the direction of the house.

Lincoln rolls his eyes, and I bite down a smile.

"That's my mum," he says.

"I guessed as much."

A tall, brunette woman speeds across the lawn until she reaches the car.

"Are these your new friends?"

Lincoln looks up at the sky and taps his foot. "Yes. This is Xander and Braden. And their mum."

She bends at the door and looks in the window. "I'm so happy to meet you. Lincoln said he'd made some new friends. I'm Alana. Alana Blake."

I beam. "Chloe Cooper."

"And you're new in town?"

I shake my head. "I grew up here. The boys are new to town, but they seem to be settling in well."

"Good to hear." She seems so friendly.

"Anyway, I've got to get these two home. I'm happy to drop Lincoln off whenever he needs a ride."

She nods. "Thank you so much."

And as I drive away, I smile to myself at the thought of cultivating that friendship.

I think it'd be good for both Xander and me.

TWENTY-ONE

HUNTER

I HATE THIS FEELING.

Maybe I could live and move on with Chloe whispering Scott's name, but she deserves to know for sure what this is between us before we take it further.

I'm all but permanently working from home now. My mood isn't good, and I'd rather not take it out on Liz or anyone else. My long-term plan was to build the company to the point where I could step back and enjoy growing old with my wife while people I trusted ran it.

But that all fell apart. Having Chloe in my life gave me new hope.

I look up at the knock on the door. It's only been a few days since I sent Chloe home, and there's no way she's already sorted out her feelings. This is going to take a while.

Piper smiles as I swing the door open, and I roll my eyes.

This is the woman who I thought I'd spend the rest of my life with—the woman who excited me so much I willingly went along with her plan that ultimately derailed our marriage. I'll never make that mistake again.

"Are you going to leave me on the doorstep?" she asks.

"It's tempting."

For a moment she studies my expression. Apart from Chloe, Piper is the woman who knows me best, but I'm not the man I was when we were together.

I step back. "I guess you should come in."

She looks around as she steps inside. "It's not changed much. I thought you would have completely redecorated."

"I never had a problem with the décor, just what happened inside the house."

She turns and smiles again.

"What do you want, Piper?"

She sucks in her top lip. "So, Chloe's back in town."

There it is. That's what triggered this. Piper was the one person who knew what, or rather who came between Scott and me. She helped me pick up the pieces when I lost my best friend, and we went from friends with benefits to husband and wife when we should never have been married in the first place.

What I thought we both wanted turned out to be an illusion, and her affair was the last straw.

"She is."

"You think you can just waltz on in and pick up Scott's leftovers. She didn't want anything to do with you back then. What makes you think she'll want you now?"

I close my eyes and take a deep breath. Piper got what she wanted in the divorce. I bought her out of the house and the business and it took until now to get back on top. I'm not about to take her shit.

"My relationship with Chloe is none of your business. Why are you even here?"

She frowns. "I do still care, Hunter, whether you believe it or not. If Chloe does let you into her life, it'll just be to fill the gap her husband left behind."

Ouch.

"Chloe's not like that."

Piper rolls her eyes. "She always thought she was better than us. And you lost your best friend because of her."

That's some deep-seated hatred right there. And while I never approved of her dislike of Chloe, her reasons were simple. She always felt second best.

But that was seventeen years ago. When I married her, I loved her. I wanted to settle down, have a family, and spend my life with her. And she wanted that too. Until she decided she didn't want children and started sleeping with the neighbour.

It was never me who gave up on us.

She's the one who remarried the minute she could. It's not like there's some lingering love story between us.

"I have a lot of regrets. But things have changed. You were wrong about Chloe then, and you're wrong about her now. Sometimes I think you only wanted me because I wanted her."

She shakes her head. "We had a lot of good years."

"And some really terrible ones. We went into a marriage that probably shouldn't have happened because we wanted different things. Maybe we should have both been more honest with each other."

Her expression straightens. I was always honest with her—I opened up about things I never shared with anyone. But our life together was built on a bed of lies.

"I wish I had been. Things might not have ended so badly between us."

"It is what it is. You have your life, and I have mine."

"Does it have to be *her*?"

I close my eyes for a moment. Any other person and I probably wouldn't have a visit from Piper. Lord knows she didn't care how many women I slept with after we split. But it's personal with Chloe.

"It can only be her." I open my eyes.

She blinks a bunch of times. "Of course."

"I'm in love with her, Piper. We're going to be together."

"So, you're not together now."

I take a deep breath. "I'm giving her some space to make sure of what she wants, but in time—"

"She's stringing you along. The way she always did." She crosses her arms.

I shake my head. "She never strung me along. She had no idea how I felt back then. But she knows now. There's been no one else in her life since Scott died. I can understand her not wanting to rush."

Her eyes tell me she's wounded, but the truth is when I was with Piper I was only with her. She made me forget the teenage crush that lost me my best friend, and I fell hard. But she never understood that no matter how many times I tried to reassure her.

And in the end, it didn't matter.

"I just don't want you to be hurt."

"There's only one woman who ever really hurt me, Piper. And it wasn't Chloe."

She looks away. I'm not about to blow smoke up her arse just because she's here showing concern.

"I should go. I just wanted to check in and make sure you were okay."

I nod. "I'll be fine."

She walks toward the door before pausing. "Call me if you need me."

Hell will freeze over first.

"Sure."

I walk out onto the front step with Piper and into the sun.

She turns, cups my face, and plants a soft kiss on my lips. "I should have been better to you, Hunter. I always knew that. But I do still care and I always will."

"Go home to your husband, Piper. I'll be fine."

She nods. "Take care."

I watch as she walks down the steps and out to the footpath before I spot something in the corner of my eye. Chloe's gaze hits me as I turn my head, and confusion fills her face before she turns and walks back toward her house.

I don't stop and correct anything about what she just saw. I'm frozen to the spot.

What I really want is to run after her and tell her I love her, and I don't care about anything else. But I don't because we can't be together if she's torn.

If we're going to do this, we both need to be committed to it. And I need to know she's committed to me. We took such big steps together, but I can't be the one who's besotted again while she's unsure of how she feels.

My choices are to rush into this and hope she falls as hard as me, or to give her breathing room to work it out herself.

I'm choosing the latter because I want to spend the rest of my life with Chloe.

And I need her to want to spend the rest of her life with me.

TWENTY-TWO

CHLOE

WHAT IF HE'S with Piper?

The thought hurts beyond all measure. I can't see Hunter letting her back into his life when she hurt him so badly, but I hurt him so much with that one little word.

There's something I always knew I needed to do before I moved on.

But everything with Hunter was so new and exciting, and I was swept away before I brought myself back to focus on why I came here in the first place—to bring Scott home.

Firing up my laptop, it doesn't take long to search for cemeteries nearby. Narrowing it down to the right place is a little more difficult, but one stands out more than the others.

"Braden. Xander. We all need to talk. Family meeting."

I sit at the kitchen table with my laptop open. We'll all need to agree on Scott's final resting place.

We do this together.

One after the other, the boys sit at the table, and Xander eyes my laptop.

"What are you doing?"

I clasp my hands, and look first at him and then at Braden. "It's time to find a home for your father. Somewhere we can go and visit when we need to talk to him. There are some beautiful spots in the town cemetery, and we can go and take a—"

"This is bullshit." Xander scrapes the floor with the chair as he pushes it back. "I know I said I was okay with you having a boyfriend, but this is a whole other level. You said we were going to keep him with us until we were all ready. And now you're making that decision for us."

"Xan, calm down," Braden says. "If this is what Mum wants ..."

"What about what I want?" Tears fill his eyes. "I'm not ready to say goodbye."

"Oh, honey. We're not saying goodbye. Not really." I stand. "What I'm saying is that we find somewhere permanent for him. Somewhere beautiful and peaceful. It's not far from here. This is what he would have wanted."

Xander breathes heavily, and I've seen him trying to control himself like this before. I know his pain. He's not really angry with me, but I'll help him through it. He's angry at the world.

"Come here." I slide my arms around my son's chest and hold him as tight as I can. "Every single day I wish things were different. I wish that none of it had happened and he was still with us." I let out a long breath. "But he's not, Xan, and he's not coming back no matter how much we want him to."

"It's not fair."

"No. None of it is fair. We have to be strong and give him his final resting place. He deserves that, and we do too." I let Xander go and cup his face. "He loved you two so much. It would break him to see how much you're hurting. But he'd also want us to find peace and move on. And this is such an important part of healing."

He gives me a short, sharp nod, and I drop my hands before returning to my seat. Xander sits back down. He's still scowling, but hopefully we've got through the worst.

"Can we go and look at the cemetery, Mum?" Braden asks.

I tilt my head a little. "Of course. We'll all go and take a look. We can choose together." I shift my gaze to Xander. "Okay?"

He doesn't respond, and I make a mental note to find a counsellor here for him. I've got a list from our doctor in Auckland, but it's a matter of finding the right one.

I should have done it when we first got here.

"Do you want to go for a drive today? We could do a little sight-seeing, grab some ice cream while we're out or something?"

"Can we get takeaways for dinner?" Xander asks.

"Sure." We've never had takeaway food so much since we've moved, but I'm happy if it helps with the whole settling process.

"Can I choose?"

"That's not fair. You chose your special rugby dinner," Braden grumps.

"Well, you two work it out between yourselves. I don't have the energy to argue with either of you right now." I close the laptop. If we're going for a drive, I already know where we need to go.

Braden just stares at me. "Maybe you should choose what we have then."

"Maybe I will."

I leave them behind in the kitchen and head upstairs to get presentable to go out.

I'm tired.

I look out the window and toward Hunter's house.

It's become clear to me that I have to work out how to move on myself before I can give him the love he so richly deserves. To give him anything less would be unfair.

He's so willing to love me and be whatever Braden and Xander need. And I need him. If I'm going to share my life with anyone, it's Hunter.

He gets me. And I know he'll share all my burdens.

I won't be alone anymore.

But I do need to make sure this is for all the right reasons and not just because I'm lonely.

IT'S PERFECT.

Here in the rose garden, surrounded by nature and plenty of sunshine is a beautiful spot for Scott. For so long, I knew what I had to do, but I didn't have the strength. Maybe part of it is knowing I can have a future without him. Before, it all seemed so bleak, even if I didn't want to admit it.

"What do you boys think?" I ask.

"I like it," Braden says.

I turn to Xander. "What about you?"

He shrugs. "Whatever."

"Xander. I want your opinion."

"I don't really know why we have to do this anyway."

I sigh. "Your dad needs a permanent resting place. We're home now, so I think this is a lovely spot for him. It's easy for us all to visit. If you really wanted to, you could walk here from school, or"—I take a deep breath—"we can get you bikes and you can ride here after school."

His head shoots up. "You'd trust us on the road by ourselves?"

"I have to some time." I rest my hand on his shoulder. "I mean, someday soon you're going to leave home, and if you leave town for uni, I can't drive you to and from there every day."

He tries not to laugh but it comes out in bursts. "I was wondering …"

"I love you and your brother more than anything in this whole world, but it's time I started treating you like the adults you are." Tears well in my eyes, and my son pulls me into his arms for a hug.

"Don't cry, Mum."

"I'm so proud of you and your brother. I know it hasn't always been easy, but I love you, and I'd do anything to keep you safe."

"I know," he murmurs.

"Let's go for a walk around and see what else is here." I loop my arm in his and lean on his shoulder.

Braden joins me on the other side, and I take hold of his arm too. "The three of us make these decisions together, okay?"

They both nod.

We make our way to a bench and sit down.

"I like it," Xander says. "You're right, it's a good place for Dad."

"Placing his ashes there doesn't mean any of us love him any less."

He nods. "I know. I just had to work it out in my head."

Braden brushes my arm. "I like it too. And we can visit whenever we want?"

"Whenever we want. I don't know about you two, but I plan on coming here to complain about everything."

Xander laughs. "You never complain."

"I'm not sure if that's true."

"We should go and get ice cream. That's what Dad would want," Braden says.

I laugh. "I think you're right. Let's get ice cream and go to the beach for a while."

He stands and grabs hold of my hand. "Come on, Mum."

I let him pull me to my feet and reach back for Xander's hand. "You too." He grins, takes my hand, and I pretend to groan as I take his weight. "I remember when you were so small I could pick you up."

"I bet I could pick you up now." He laughs.

"Bet you couldn't."

I laugh as Xander plucks me up off the ground and spins me around.

"That's not fair." I lean against him as he puts me back down.

"Love you, Mum."

"I love you too."

TWENTY-THREE

HUNTER

"GO HOME, HUNTER."

I look up and eye Liz, standing in the doorway.

"Huh?"

"You're like a bear with a sore head. All you've done is whinge all morning. Go home to work and leave me alone."

I chuckle. "I can't be that bad."

"I'm not sure what's going on with you, but I don't want you here when you're grumpy."

I stand, pick up my jacket, and walk toward the door. "Who made you the boss?"

"You did." She laughs, and all I can do is smile.

"I'm sorry."

"You really have it bad for this woman."

I narrow my gaze. "How did you ..."

"Nothing's got you so messed up since your divorce. I hope it works out the way you want it to."

"Me too."

I leave the building and climb into the car. Chloe's been on my mind since the night I told her to leave, and it's interfering with everything. I love her, and I want to be with her. But I can't be second best.

She's out the front of her house when I arrive home, and I catch my breath at the sight of her. I'm not even sure if I should wave or not, but as I park the car, she walks toward me, covering the short distance between our places and striding up the driveway.

"I'm glad I caught you."

Hope wells in my chest.

"It's good to see you, Chlo."

She smiles. "You too. I just wanted to let you know that we found a place for Scott's ashes. We'll be having a small ceremony to place them, and I thought you might like to be there."

I nod. "I would. Thank you for thinking of me."

"You meant a lot to him, Hunter. I'm not making it public. It'll just be family. And no matter what, you're family."

Swallowing down the lump in my throat, I force a smile. It's so hard to be tough on her, but I can't back down. Being with Chloe is my dream, but it has to be the real deal and not some half-arsed approximation. "That means a lot." I bite my lip. "This isn't because of us, is it? I don't want you doing this if you're not ready."

She draws in a breath while dropping eye contact. "Maybe a little. But the truth is, this is something I should have done a while ago. It's not healthy to keep holding on. We just had to be in the right place, and we are now."

I want to hold her. I want to take her in my arms and protect her from what's to come. It doesn't take a genius to know this will be a hugely emotional time for her and her boys. All I want to do is protect the three of them and shelter them from the storm.

This is such a big step for all of them.

"Chloe, about us ..."

She shakes her head. "You were right. I need to work out my own world before I let you into it. Anything less isn't fair on you." She closes her eyes and exhales a long breath. "That's if you still want in."

Her eyes are tear-filled when she opens them. I did this. I could have so easily told her Piper's visit wasn't what she probably thought it was. All she saw was Piper kiss me goodbye, but it's enough to have rocked her faith in me.

"I want in. I want everything."

She gives me a small smile. "I hope so."

"Come here." I open my arms to her and she falls into them. She smells of fresh air and sunshine. I know she's been out in the pool a lot while the weather's nice. I've not been watching her but have heard the splash of water and the sounds of music drifting toward me.

"I miss you," she whispers.

"I miss you too." I kiss the top of her head. "And I'm right here and waiting when you're ready. I always will be."

She squeezes me tight and then steps away. "I'll text you the details of the interment."

Reaching out, I run my thumb down her cheek. Tears spill from her eyes and I catch one on the end of my thumb. "I'll be there."

"I'm so sorry I hurt you."

I shake my head. "I'm a big boy. You know how I feel about you. I just have to be patient."

She sucks on her bottom lip. How I want to kiss those tears away and forget any of this ever happened.

"Xander gave us his approval," she says.

That makes me smile. "You told him?"

"He came to me and told me he likes you. That I should invite you over more."

I nod slowly. "That sounds good to me."

She comes forward again, pecks me on the cheek and then disappears back next door.

I watch her go with so much regret, but every step she takes is one closer to us being together.

What I need to do is keep my faith in her.

TWENTY-FOUR

CHLOE

"MUM, HURRY UP."

"I'm coming," I call out.

The morning has been crap. I woke up late, and I'm not feeling that great as I walk into my en-suite to give my hair a quick brush.

Pulling open the vanity drawer, I lay eyes on a packet of tampons. I haven't replaced these since we moved in.

I'm not unaccustomed to my period not turning up. I've found since Scott died that stress plays a big part in it. They were very erratic at one point but settled over time. But now that's happened right along with my exhaustion, which I also put down to stress.

What if it's not?

I've only ever felt this awful one time in my life, and I ended up with twins eight months later.

Surely not.

No.

"Mum." I'm too tired to even work out which twin is calling, but I grab my brush and flick it through my hair, glad for the millionth time that I had it cut shorter. It's so much easier to manage.

"We're going to be late." Braden taps his foot.

"We're fine. Get in the car."

"Mum, do you know where my rugby gear is? I know you washed it," Xander asks.

"It's already in your bag," I snap.

"Oh, thanks, Mum." He recoils, and I immediately regret my tone.

"Sorry for being grumpy. I'm just tired this morning. Let's get going."

I've never been so relieved as I drop them at the school gate.

MY PHONE RINGS as I drive toward the supermarket, and I press the answer button on the steering wheel.

"Hi, Meredith," I say, reading the screen.

"Where are you off to in such a hurry?" she asks.

"What? Where are you?"

She laughs. "I waved at you about two minutes ago, and you zoomed straight past me. I just picked up a coffee from that cafe we went to."

I lick my lips. "I'm just running errands."

"Want to hang out? Come 'round to my place. The kids are at school and Darren's away on business for the week. I could do with some company."

I swallow hard. Maybe this friendship with Meredith is what I need right now. She's kept my relationship with Hunter quiet, but can I trust her with this? I can't do this alone. I'm not sure if my mother could deal with me being pregnant, and Caleb would just want to kill Hunter.

"That sounds great. I'll grab what I need from the supermarket and pop over to your place. Do you need anything?"

"No. I've got a full pantry, and we can watch a trashy movie or something."

I smile. "That works for me. See you in about half an hour."

Ending the call as I drive into the car park, I sigh.

What the hell do I do if I am pregnant? *One thing at a time.* If I'm not, and it's a false alarm, then no harm. If I am, it adds another layer of complication.

Walking down the aisles, I grab a few other things before I reach the aisle with the pregnancy tests. I pick up the test off the shelf. There are two in the pack, one to check and one to confirm the result I guess.

"What do we do if it's positive?" I ask Scott.

He leans his head on my shoulder. "Then, I guess we're having a baby."

"Are we really ready for this?"

"I'm not sure anyone's ever ready for it, Chloe. But we've got each other, and that's all that matters to me."

That was a lifetime ago, and a very different situation. But now, as then, I need to test to find the result.

Getting myself together, I throw the test kit in the trolley and make my way to the checkout.

It's time to go and find out.

"CHLOE." Meredith beams as she opens the door. "I'm so glad you said yes. I have been going round the twist by myself this week. But I know you're a busy lady."

"I'm never too busy for you. Just call me if you need company. I can work from anywhere."

"Come in."

I kick off my shoes and step foot inside her living room. "I'm actually really glad you called. There's something I need to do."

"Anything you need, it's yours." She smiles.

"I just need a friend to hold my hand while I do this." I hold up the pregnancy test.

Her mouth falls open. "Really?"

"I don't know." I shrug. "It's been a while."

"Are you and Hunter still ..."

"Not right now. We kind of broke up."

Confusion crosses her face. "Why?"

I bite my bottom lip. "I called out Scott's name in bed."

"Oh, Chloe." Her expression fills with sympathy. "Surely that's understandable.'

"Hunter deserves better." I sigh. "And there are things I need to take care of before I can really be ready for a relationship with him."

"Like what?"

I swallow hard. "I got so carried away with what we were doing, I neglected the things I came here for. Like finding Scott a final resting place."

"Oh, Chloe." She places her hand on mine. "He'd want you to be happy no matter what."

"I know. It's just ... I need to make sure Hunter gets a hundred per cent of me. It's not fair on him otherwise."

She gestures toward the test. "And if that's positive?"

"Then I need to take a breath and work things out before I tell him. Because you know Hunter, he'll settle because he wants to do the right thing when he shouldn't settle."

"Being with you would never be settling for him. Don't you know that?"

I shrug. "Maybe, but *I* can't do that to him. I need time."

She grips my hand. "Whatever happens today is between you and me. I hope you know that."

"Thanks, Meredith."

"Go and take that test and put yourself out of your misery. I've got you. If it's positive, then we'll kick back and I'll make popcorn. If it's negative, we'll crack open a bottle of wine."

I laugh. "I can't do that. I've got to pick up the boys later."

"Okay. We'll save that for another time. At least I made you laugh. Now, go."

RESULTS IN THREE MINUTES.

Seventeen years ago, give or take a few months, those were the longest three minutes of my life. I was so young and just starting my adult life. Now I've been an adult for so long, but again at a point in my life when I'm starting out.

And now I have to wait another three minutes.

Last time, I had Scott by my side waiting for the results. Today, I'm glad to have Meredith. I'm not sure I'd have the strength to do this alone.

And I can't risk hurting Hunter even more by turning to him with this only for it to be negative.

Hell, I'm not even sure how I feel about it all.

I pace back and forward, staring at the patterned rug under the coffee table.

"If you don't sit down, you'll wear my carpet out. It won't be much longer," Meredith says.

With a sigh, I drop down onto the couch beside her, and fan my face with my hand. "It's so hot in here."

She nudges my arm. "It's not. You're just freaking out."

"I think I'm allowed to." I bury my face in my hands.

"Let's take a look. Put you out of your misery."

"I can't. What does it say?" I peek between my fingers.

Meredith's expression is blank. "Chloe, you're pregnant."

Nausea sweeps over me.

Hunter was right. I did need to find myself. And these past few weeks I've felt more like Chloe than I have in years.

But now this.

Tears well in my eyes. I wanted more children at different stages in my life, but now feels like a terrible time. I'm right in the middle of reclaiming myself, and I don't want this to be the reason Hunter and I are forced back together.

"It's okay. We'll work it out. You've got me." Meredith rubs my shoulder. "I'm here if you need anything. And I won't tell a soul."

"Thank you. I'm sorry for the tears."

"Want some tissues?"

I nod, sniffing as the tears roll down my cheeks.

She opens a drawer in the coffee table and pulls out a box that she thrusts at me.

"Scott and I talked about having more children, but the twins were so much work in the early days, and then it just never happened."

Meredith's eyes well up, and she grabs for a tissue. "Maybe this was just meant to be. Maybe it's a sign that you and Hunter belong together."

I wipe my face before blowing my nose. "Maybe. I just know I need to do a lot of thinking."

Her smile's small, but she's trying to show her support, and I appreciate it more than anything.

"Well, I'm always here. Give me a call any time."

"Thank you. You and Darren will come to Scott's interment, won't you? I just have to finalise the details, but it'll be next week."

She nods. "We'll be there."

TWENTY-FIVE

CHLOE

MY LURCHING stomach wakes me up.

The alarm plays music beside me, and my blurry eyes take in the time: 7:48.

Shit.

I've completely overslept on a weekday for the first time ever.

Dragging myself out of bed, I pull on my bathrobe and make my way down the stairs. Braden and Xander both turn to stare at me as I trudge into the room, yawning.

"We weren't sure about waking you up," Braden says.

"I'm not sure how I slept in, but I'm here now. If you're ready, I'll get dressed."

"Uncle Caleb's on his way. We called him so you could rest." He studies me closely. "Are you okay?"

I breathe out a sigh of relief as my stomach roils. I can't remember morning sickness being this bad with the twins, but I was also seventeen years younger when I went through a pregnancy before.

"I'm sure it's just a stomach bug. I'll be fine." I force a smile.

He takes a step toward me and comes to a stop. "I won't hug you. I don't want your bug."

I laugh. "That's fine. Are you ready for school?"

"Nearly." Xander's expression is just as concerned. I don't get sick very often, so they're both worried. I just have to find a way to alleviate those fears.

My heart races at a sudden thump to the door. *Caleb.*

"I'll go and let him in," Xander says.

He disappears for a moment and comes back with Caleb trailing behind him.

"What's up with you? You look like shit." Caleb runs his gaze over me.

"Just a stomach bug. Some sleep, and I'll be fine."

He shifts his focus to the boys. "Go grab your things and let's get going. I'll pick you up too so your mother can have a break."

They both bolt out of the room while he grasps my arm. "Are you sure you're okay?"

I rub his hand. "I will be if I can get some rest. Thank you for coming."

"Any time you need me, I'm here. It's just not like you to be sick."

"I know, but I'd appreciate you not making a big deal about it because it'll just worry the boys."

He bows his head. "Understood."

"Ready." Braden appears, followed by Xander. They pick up their bags and head back out the door.

Caleb plants a kiss on my cheek. "I'll drop them off safe and sound after school."

"Thank you."

With a kiss to each cheek, my children leave the house.

The door closes and I'm left by myself.

Having children is funny. There are times when all you want is to be by yourself, but when they're gone, you just want them to come back.

But I have to get used to them being around less and less.

Although now it seems I won't be alone for long.

IT'S mid-afternoon when I finally get out of bed.

I strip out of my clothes and put my bikini on. Screw work for the day. I'll regret it later, but the sun is shining outside, and I want to make the most of the good weather before it begins to cool.

Grabbing a towel from the cupboard, I head out to the pool. The autumn sun warms my skin, and I take deep breaths of the fresh air.

I do love this place.

Despite questioning myself when we first got here, I'm settled now. I'll still have the memories, but they don't hit me as hard as they initially did. Besides, Scott will always be with me no matter how much time passes or where his ashes are.

I lie back on the sun lounger and different memories hit me.

"You were the one with hands all over me the other morning."

"You were the one who slept in my bed."

Instinctively, I rest my hand on my stomach. The timing's not right for this baby, but when will it be? The twins didn't have their timing right either, but they're my whole world. I can't even contemplate life without them. And this baby will be the same. Maybe we'll have the girl I always wanted. And there's a big age gap, but I know Braden and Xander will love this child whether it's a girl or a boy. Hunter and I will too.

I just need to work out how to tell him.

I'm sure he'll be happy. He said he wanted kids. But I know he'll also be wary of me, and while I understand it, that thought hurts.

I drop my sunglasses down and look up at his window. There's no sign of movement—I don't even know if he's home. He said he'd wait, but I'm still none the wiser about Piper's visit. I'm not even sure right now if it's any of my business.

Being an adult returning to single life is hard. Especially when you haven't been through it as a young person.

I'm as confused as ever.

"Mum?" Xander's voice carries out into the back yard.

"Out here," I call.

His brow is furrowed as he approaches. "Are you feeling better?"

"Much. Just getting some sun. How was your day?"

He smiles, and it's like the day just got warmer. "Good. I might go and get changed and come back down for a swim. Can we get takeaways for dinner?"

I laugh. "Sure. I don't really feel like cooking tonight. Anything you want in particular?"

He shrugs. "I'll talk to Braden."

I sigh as he disappears back inside. Today was a good day for Xander, and maybe me letting go a little this morning has helped.

Every small step we take seems to be a huge leap to something better.

TWENTY-SIX
CHLOE

I ALWAYS THOUGHT my life was blessed.

Our early years with the twins were tough. We had no money, but we had all the love. And we managed to keep our heads above water, even though it was hard.

We emerged as a family who could tackle anything.

Until the worst possible thing happened.

That was one of the hardest days of my life.

The funeral was awful. Surrounded by family and friends, I felt completely alone. The other half of me was gone, and I was helpless to do anything about it.

Seeing his ashes lain to rest isn't as bad, but it's still rough.

My heart is heavy as the box containing him is placed in the ground. I thought I'd said goodbye, but really I just delayed it until now.

To my left, a hand slides into mine and grips it tight. I turn my head to see Braden looking at me. Xander appears on the other side, and both boys effectively hold me up while I watch the interment of my husband's ashes.

I breathe in deep and exhale through my mouth to keep myself under control.

There are words said, but I barely hear them as I focus on that small hole in the ground. A piece of my heart is sealed in there with him as they close it up. There's more work to do, but the plaque is put on top so we can see it as it will be.

Afterward, all I feel is numb, but it's done now and I know healing will come from this. It's just a matter of time, as it always is.

There's no wake. We had one for the funeral, and I didn't want this day to drag on longer than it has to. And when it's done, everyone steps back and leaves my boys and I alone. It's nice to have the quiet with them for a moment.

"Goodbye, Dad," Xander whispers.

I grip his hand tight. "He'll always be with us."

"I know." He gives me a small smile.

"Mum?"

I turn to Braden. "Yes?"

"We're just going to go and talk to Uncle Caleb."

I nod.

Caleb's just a short distance from me, and he winks as I make eye contact. With the boys out of the way, Hunter moves closer.

"Thank you for inviting me," he says.

I shuffle from one foot to the other. "You're welcome."

His gaze drops on my mouth. *Is he thinking about kissing me? I want him to*. I want him to take me in his arms and make me forget today ever happened.

But that's not fair on either one of us.

"I'm glad you came."

He nods. "I couldn't be anywhere else today. For you or your boys. How are you all doing?"

I look down at my shoes, kicking my toe into the dirt. "Xander was a little angry that we were doing it to start with, but he understands."

"It must be confusing."

Meeting his gaze again, tears prick my eyes. "It is, but I think this will give us all some closure we should have had a long time ago."

He reaches out and cups my cheek. It's an unexpected, intimate move, and for a fleeting moment, all I can think about is how many eyes must be on us.

"You're so much stronger than you even realise. Just remember that whatever happens between us, we'll always be friends. I'm here for you and your family."

I grasp his wrist. "Thank you."

For a moment, we just look at each other, and it feels good—it feels right.

"I'll just go and pay my respects to your brother and your boys. See you later?"

I nod. "I'd like that."

He walks away. I take two steps only to be confronted by Kay.

"Is there something you have to tell me about Hunter?"

I raise my eyebrows. "Why?"

Regardless of her being my mother-in-law, my personal life is none of her business. And this is the one thing I worried about coming home. She's very keen to stick her nose into anything that makes me look bad.

She always thought I dragged Scott down when I became pregnant, and urged him to 'send me home' when home was always with him. It caused a rift between them, but not to the point of wrecking their relationship completely.

"You looked very cosy."

"Hunter's an old friend, of mine and Scott's."

She nods. "Anything you do impacts the boys. I hope you know that."

My blood begins to boil. Everything I've done my entire adult life has centred around my children. She was never there for us in any meaningful way.

Braden bounds toward me. "Mum, Hunter offered to take us for a burger while you finish up here. Is that okay?"

I turn away from Kay and smile at him. "Of course you can. I won't be much longer. See you at home."

"I'll make sure he gets something for you." Braden bends and kisses me on the cheek.

"Thank you."

For a moment, I watch him and Xander follow Hunter to his car. Hunter's timing couldn't be better, so I suppress the urge to smile.

Instead, I take a deep breath and turn back to Kay. "Thank you for your concern, but I'm sure you can see the boys and I are fine. They're always my first priority."

Her expression darkens. I'm not sure how to win with her. I've been on the back foot since I was eighteen. She and I got on great for years, but once we hit trouble, she rarely gave me an inch. Distance helped, but now that advantage is gone.

"Kay, I brought Scott home for all of us. It's where he needed to be. And now we can all visit him, and it'll give the boys some sense of closure. They need it more than anyone—even me."

At that, she seems lost for words. I know she lost a son when I lost a husband, but there's a lot I had to battle through alone, and I did. And for the first time, I think I've been able to stop, take a breath, and see how tough it really did make me.

Through it all, I never let her see that it wasn't always wonderful between Scott and myself. We had our tough times just like every other couple, but we always emerged stronger, and I might not have been able to say goodbye, but my husband died knowing just how much I loved him, and I knew the same.

She's not going to cut me down now.

Kay gives me a short, sharp nod. Today is not the day to fight with her, but it's hard not to get defensive. I don't love Scott less for giving him a final resting place. It's one of the hardest things I've ever had to do, and I won't be made to feel guilty for feeling again.

"Chloe, are you going home or do you want to come to Mum and Dad's for a while?"

I breathe a sigh of relief as Caleb strolls toward us. It's a welcome distraction, as I know he's done some garden work for Kay and her husband, and she likes him.

"I'm going home. I just want to have a lie down after today."

His dark eyes are so full of affection. "Fair enough." He gestures toward Kay. "Mrs Cooper."

"Caleb. I hope you're doing well." She gives him a smile that I'd never get, and all it does is get my back up.

"I'm doing great now I have my sister home." He shoots me a wink and I look away in amusement.

"I'm sure. Keep in touch, Chloe. We'd love to see the boys soon."

I bite my tongue as she walks away.

"You're welcome," Caleb says. "I saw the boys head out with Hunter."

I nod. "He's taking them for a burger."

"Someone's got a crush," he sings, and I glare at him. "Oh. It's not just one-sided, is it?"

"It's complicated, and I'm not talking about it today." I poke my tongue at him.

He chuckles. "You could do a lot worse. He's a good guy."

I grin. "He is, but how do you know? You've met him once."

"We've already had the talk where I asked him what his intentions are."

A part of me dies inside of embarrassment. "What?"

"Well, clearly I didn't scare him off." He laughs. "Relax, Chloe. You should see your face right now. It's priceless."

My cheeks burn. "I can't believe you talked to him like that."

He reaches out and grips my shoulder. "You'd better believe that I'm watching out for my little sister. I'm glad you're home, and I just want you to be happy."

"Thanks, big bro."

"I'll leave you to it. Catch up with you later?"

I nod. "Just come over during the day some time. I'm always home."

He bends and plants a kiss on my cheek. "I'll do that. Love you."

"Love you too."

And all of a sudden, I'm beside Scott's grave by myself.

Adored husband of Chloe. Loved father of Braden and Xander.

Those few words bring tears to my eyes, as they're not enough to describe what he was to us, but they're a clear message to the rest of the world.

"I love you, Scott. I did the best I could, and I hope you're happy here. I'll visit, and the boys will too." I kneel beside the plaque. "There will never be a day that I don't wish you were here, but I have to find a way to make a new life without you. And that's so damn hard."

Tears flood my vision.

"I'm pregnant, and it's Hunter's. I think I love him, Scott, and I wanted him so much, but we rushed into something, and now I'm having a baby. That's the first time I've said that out loud." I laugh through the tears. "Ironically, the one person I could always confide in is you, and you're not exactly going to give me any advice. But I'd like to think you'd just be happy for me, whatever happens."

I kiss my fingertips and press them to his name. "See you soon."

I'm so glad the boys are with Hunter—I wouldn't want them to see me break down as I'm sitting in the car trying to get myself together to drive home. And I have to make sure I'm absolutely together before I do that.

I grab a box of tissues from the glovebox and blow my nose, throwing the used ones on the passenger seat to get rid of when I'm home. The tears that stain my cheeks are next, and I look at myself in the rear view mirror until the redness around my eyes subsides a little and I'm calm again.

Driving away is right up there with the toughest things I've ever done in my life.

But it's time to go.

PARKED IN MY DRIVEWAY, I check the mirror again before I get out of the car.

It's plain to see I've been crying, but I don't look as bad as I did back at the cemetery.

It'll do.

I open the door into the kitchen, and what I see warms my heart.

Hunter sits at the dining table with Braden and Xander. All three of them are eating, talking, and laughing, and I end up on the verge of tears again.

"Mum." Braden looks up. He frowns, and I'm sure it's because my face is still a mess.

"Hey, guys. You look like you're having fun."

"Hunter let us choose whatever we wanted. And we got you your McChicken combo." Xander smiles. I thought he'd struggle more today, but apparently having your favourite takeaway meal helps.

"Sounds great."

Hunter stands. "I'll heat it up."

"I can get it."

"No. Get off your feet. That's an order. It's been a long day for you."

"Thanks, Hunter. For everything."

His warm smile makes everything better. "You're welcome."

"Are you okay?" Braden asks as I sit down beside him.

I draw a deep breath. "I will be. It's just been a very tiring day. I hope you two are alright."

"I'm glad Dad's under the trees there. It's a nice place," Xander says.

I nod. "It's beautiful. I think he'd approve."

Behind me, the microwave beeps, and Hunter places a plate in front of me with a steaming burger and fries. At first, the scent makes me nauseous, but then hunger comes out of nowhere, and I just know the burger won't be enough.

"Thank you. Again."

He chuckles as he sits. “I’m just happy to help out. I know what an emotional time this must be for you.”

“It is, but he’s home now.”

“Hunter said he’d play cricket with us when we’ve finished eating.” Xander meets my gaze.

“Did he? That’s great.”

Hunter smiles. “As long as no one breaks any windows.”

“You could play too if you want.” Xander might be inviting me, but he knows cricket’s not my forte.

His heart is in the right place.

“I think I’m going to eat this and then have a nap.” I stifle a yawn. “Maybe another day.”

“I’m going to get the gear out of the shed,” he says.

Braden stands. “I’ll help set up.”

“See you outside, Hunter.”

With the boys gone, Hunter and I are left alone in the kitchen. He reaches for my hand. “I hope I’m not overstepping any mark doing this with the kids.”

I shake my head. “No. They’re letting you in, and it’s doing my heart good to see.”

“I’m glad.” He smiles, but it’s sad and wistful. “I still hope one day that we can be a family.”

“I can’t think of anyone I’d rather share a family with than you.” The words are on the tip of my tongue. I could so easily tell him, and I will, but I’m not sure today is the right day. Besides, the last thing I want is to rush again into something and still not quite be ready.

I’ll have to tell him soon, but right now I need to work this out in my head.

He leans over and presses a long kiss to my forehead. “One day, Chloe, I’ll make all your dreams come true. Every single one. Especially the dreams that got stopped short. Anything you need, I’ll give it to you.”

“Don’t you dare make me cry. I’ve had enough of that for today,” I whisper.

"When you're ready, and we're together, and I know we will be—I swear I'll never make you cry."

I slide my arms around his neck and he kisses my lips softly.

"Hunter," Braden calls.

"I'd better get going before they come in and find me kissing their mum." He plants a kiss by my ear. "Love you."

And then he's gone, but he's playing such an important role in my boys' lives right now and hasn't really gone anywhere.

He's trying in his own way to show me what our life could be like.

And it will be.

One day.

I YAWN AGAIN as I make my way up the stairs and into my bedroom.

This is my new normal. Nausea in the morning and exhaustion in the afternoon, but today is much worse. Today, I'm not just physically exhausted but mentally as well.

I'm still glad we did it. However hard it was, Scott's resting place is permanent, and every step I take leads me to a more independent life away from the old. As it has to be.

I close my eyes.

When I open them again, I raise my left hand to look at the rings on my finger. The engagement ring isn't even the first ring Scott bought me. We'd just had the boys and were exhausted from getting no sleep from endless feeding and nappies. He bought me a costume jewellery cubic zirconia with a promise that, one day, he'd buy me the real deal.

It wasn't until our fifth wedding anniversary that we traded up. The first ring sits in my jewellery box, never forgotten.

Now these two other rings will join it. It's time.

I let out a shaky breath as I slide them from my fingers. I'm not sure how long the tracks that have been worn into my skin will last.

But as I drop the rings into the jewellery box, it's as if a weight has lifted from my chest.

The realisation that I have to take control of my life is a difficult one, but true. These are only the first steps to finding my way back to *me*.

Hunter's on my mind the whole time, but he's not the entire reason for doing this. The counsellor the boys saw told me there were things we had to let go of to move on, but we were all so resistant and set in our ways.

It's not just me I'm doing these things for. It's for Braden and Xander. They deserve their mother to be whole, and deserve the same for themselves.

I strip down to my underwear, tug on Hunter's shirt, and climb into bed.

Closing my eyes is the last thing I remember.

I wake when the bed dips beside me.

"Mum," Braden whispers.

I chuckle as he slides into bed.

"Yes?"

"Nothing. Just wanted to see if you were awake. Goodnight, Mum."

I grin, letting out a sigh as my other son appears on the other side of my bed. Shuffling over, I leave room for Xander. After today, I'm not surprised to see them, but I'd also bet this will be the last time.

While I feel lighter, I think a collective weight has been lifted from all of us.

TWENTY-SEVEN

CHLOE

WHEN THEY WERE LITTLE, Braden and Xander used to have sleepovers with their friends. I hated being apart from them, but I knew it was just a part of growing up.

Scott's death stopped that. We all just wanted to be together.

It does my heart good that Xander's friend, Lincoln invited them over to stay on Saturday night. But it still makes my stomach clench as I drop them off outside his house because it'll be the first night in four years I haven't been nearby. Even the nights I stayed at Hunter's house, I was never far away.

Xander pops a kiss on my cheek before grabbing the giant bag of popcorn we just picked up at the supermarket and stepping out of the car.

"Hey," I say.

He turns back and ducks his head into the door. "What?"

"I'm proud of you. Have fun."

"Bye, Mum." Braden leans forward and kisses the back of my head.

"Have a good night, you two. Be good for Mrs Blake."

For a moment, I just sit and watch as they make their way up the front path. Lincoln opens the door, and with a final wave from Braden, they disappear inside.

We didn't talk much on the way, but the car seems so quiet in their wake. But I have to head home and wait for them to let me know when they're ready in the morning.

It'll be weird being by myself tonight.

AFTER A DINNER FOR ONE, I swim until the light begins to fade.

Ever since that day I broke down out here, I've found the pool calming. Maybe it's because the thoughts that conjured up those memories that day hurt but also bring me comfort.

Scott would love this place. And I'd like to think he'd be happy to know we're right next to Hunter.

Hunter, who will always be there for my family, no matter what.

Hunter, who *is* family.

I pull myself out of the pool and dry off before heading inside. After a warm shower, I pull on one of Hunter's shirts and a baggy pair of trackpants.

It's when I head back into the kitchen that the phone rings out.

"Mum." I know it's Xander because of the caller ID, but I can barely recognise his voice. I've never heard it shake so much, even with him saying one word.

"What's wrong?"

"There was an accident. Braden—"

My legs fail and I fall to the floor. Whatever else he says disappears with the rushing sound of blood in my ears.

"Mum."

"What happened?" I manage to get out the words.

"We were in a car accident. Some guy did CPR on Braden. He's got a head injury and it's bad. We're in the hospital. Mum, I'm so sorry. We screwed up."

"I ... I'm on my way."

Grabbing my bag and my keys, I head out to the car.

My hand shakes so hard, I can't even get the key in the ignition.

There's no way I can drive.

Hunter.

I don't even know if he's home, but I have to take the chance. This is all my fault. I took my eye off the ball as far as my boys are concerned. I can't lose Braden.

I can't.

I fling open the door and run along the footpath and into Hunter's front yard. Running up the front steps, I hammer on the door.

The hall light flicks on.

"Just a minute."

A minute seems like hours as I wait for him.

"Hunter. Please."

He flings open the door, confusion all over his face. "Chloe? What's wrong?"

"The boys were in an accident. I need to get to the hospital."

He steps through the door, takes my car keys from my hand, and locks the door behind him. "Let's go."

He doesn't hesitate. He doesn't even ask me what kind of accident.

I try and keep pace, running behind him back to my abandoned car in the driveway. Flinging open the passenger door, I get in as he climbs into the driver's side. He starts the car and backs out of the driveway, and for the millionth time I'm so thankful to have him in my life.

"What happened?" he asks.

"The boys went for a movie night and sleepover with a friend. Xander called me from the hospital to say they'd been in a car accident."

I know my voice is getting louder, and my hands shake again as I speak.

"Chloe, you need to calm down. I know you're stressed, but this isn't going to do you any good."

I nod, open the glove box, and pull out a tissue. "I'm so sorry. I couldn't drive myself."

He glances at me. "You're family. You never need to apologise."

"I'm pregnant."

Silence falls over us, and his jaw tightens as we drive in the semi darkness.

"You're pregnant." He says it so quietly.

"I didn't mean to tell you that way. I wanted to find the right time. But my head is so full of crazy thoughts and ..."

"Chloe." His tone is so soft. "We'll talk about it later. Let's just make sure our boy is okay."

Our boy.

Tears prick my eyes. I never asked Hunter to be the father of my children—Scott's children. Just having him in their life is enough. But that one word changes everything. And where I might have felt awkward about it if he'd said it earlier, it does seem perfect now.

"I love you."

Hunter glances at me. "Took you long enough."

He's right. I just had to get my head and my heart aligned and let go of the past. I didn't need to let go of Scott to do that—he'll always be with me.

But Hunter's my future. He always was.

He grabs hold of my hand across the centre console, and his warmth flows through me in that reassuring way only Hunter has.

I take in deep breaths as we draw closer to the hospital. It's the longest drive of my life, and relief washes over me as Hunter pulls up right beside where Xander's standing.

"I'll park the car and come back." He squeezes my hand.

"Thank you."

He leans over and gives me a tender kiss before letting go.

I open the door and step out. "Xander."

His face. It's been four years since I last saw his expression so full of pain. Braden and Xander have always had a link that no one else could ever be a part of.

"I don't even know what happened. It was all so quick. Lincoln was driving fast and we both told him not to and then ..."

"Lincoln was driving? Why did you go anywhere? Where was his mother?"

His gaze drops right along with my heart. "Don't be mad, Mum."

"Answer me."

"We just wanted to get more food. Mrs Blake is away for the weekend. Lincoln said he'd driven his mum's car before. He's on his restricted license."

I draw in a deep breath. "Let me get this straight. You two lied to me. And now your brother's in this hospital with a head injury."

He swallows hard and nods.

"I can't ... Let's just get inside and see how he is."

We walk in to Accident and Emergency, and I head straight to the reception.

"I'm Braden Cooper's mother," I say to the lady behind the desk.

She nods, flicking a glance at Xander. "I'll find someone to help you. Take a seat."

I grab hold of Xander's hand and squeeze. "Thank you."

Sitting on the nearest chair, I tap my foot impatiently on the ground.

"Mum, I'm sorry."

"I know you are." I'm not even sure I can look at him right now. "Are you okay?"

"Just a few bumps and bruises. We got brought straight here in an ambulance. I called you as soon as I could."

"The hospital should have called me."

My phone rings in my bag, and I pull it out. It's a number I don't recognise.

"Mrs Cooper?"

"Are you ringing to tell me my sons have been in an accident?"

There's a pause. "Yes."

"I'm sitting waiting in Accident and Emergency to see Braden. Xander's with me."

"I'll get someone to come and see you."

I hang up the call without a care if I'm being rude. I'm just glad Xander called me when he did, even if I haven't seen Braden yet.

"Hey," Hunter arrives and sits on the other side of Xander. "How's Braden?"

"I don't know yet. I'm waiting."

He reaches over to touch my arm. "I'm not going anywhere. You know that, right?"

I nod. "I know. Thank you."

"Mrs Cooper?"

I look up to see a nurse standing in front of me.

"Yes? How is he?"

"He's stable, but if you could please come with me and the doctor will speak with you. Just one of you at this stage."

As I stand, Xander stands too. I turn toward him. "Stay here with Hunter."

"But, Mum ..."

"Hey, mate. Your mum has to go and deal with this, and I'll wait with you." Hunter puts his hand on Xander's arm.

"Thank you." I've said it what feels a million times, but it still feels inadequate.

He meets my gaze. "Go, Chloe."

And then I'm off down the corridor, following a nurse to see my eldest son. I never got to say goodbye to his father. I just pray I don't have to say goodbye to Braden.

I'm not sure I can survive a second loss, and I know Xander can't.

Braden has to get better.

HE'S BREATHING.

His eyes are closed, but his chest rises and falls and it's enough to bring tears to my eyes.

"Braden," I whisper.

"Mrs Cooper." I turn to see a man in a white coat. "I'm Doctor Kirwan."

"How's my son?"

"He's stable, but we will have to relieve some of the pressure in his head. So, there will be surgery tonight."

I nod. "I understand."

"He's very lucky, Mrs Cooper. The other boy in the front of the car ..."

I look up. "Lincoln?"

The doctor nods. "He didn't make it."

I let out a gasp. He might not be my child, but pain rips through me at the thought of his parents being told about his death.

I've seen the police car in my driveway.

I've had them knock on my door.

"Mrs Cooper?"

"My husband. Braden's father. He died the same way."

Understanding crosses his expression. "I'm sorry to hear that."

"Thank you for taking care of my son."

"You're welcome. There are always risks with surgery ..."

I give him a stiff nod. "I know. But I also know he's in the right place. Please do your best."

He gives me a small smile. "His chances are very, very good, Mrs Cooper. He'll be in the best of hands. The nurse will let you know when we're ready for him."

"Thank you. Can my son and ... partner come and sit with me? Braden and Xander are identical twins, and Xander will be anxious."

"Yes of course. That should be fine. I'll get them shown through."

"Thanks. I appreciate it."

And then for a moment, I'm left alone with my son.

I sit on a chair beside the bed and take Braden's hand in mine. The machine monitoring his heart rate beeps steadily, and it gives me some comfort right along with hearing him breathe.

"Hang in there, sweetheart." I swallow hard. "I love you."

TWENTY-EIGHT

HUNTER

MY JAW TICS with impatience as I wait for Chloe to come back with some news.

This was always so much more than just her and me. These boys mean the world to me, and have done since the first day we met. It's never been the two of us, it's meant to be the four of us.

Five.

My hands tremble so I rub them together. When Chloe mentioned she was pregnant, I didn't quite let it sink in.

The start to our romance was messy. We went straight to sex and worked backward. But she's still Chloe, the girl I fell in love with—the woman I want to be with.

"So ... you and my mum?" Xander steadies his gaze on me.

I nod. "We were going to tell you. She just wanted a little time to get used to the idea. A new relationship is a big step for her."

"We're fine with it. We both like you. And she smiles when you're around." He looks down at his feet. "Like really smiles. She hasn't done that since before Dad died."

"I want to make her happy"—I pause—"And the two of you.

Don't think that because your mum and I are together that you'll be left out. You're her everything."

He looks back up, tears welling in his eyes. "Do you think Braden will be okay?"

It's a tough question to answer when you don't know what's going on.

"I hope so, bud. You're all tough. You've been through a lot. We just have to believe."

He shuffles toward me. "I can't lose him. Mum can't ..."

"Come here."

Xander moves over until he's seated next to me, and I slide my arm around his shoulder. "We all have to look after each other right now, and be there, whatever happens. I'm not going anywhere."

His nod is short and sharp. "Thank you."

"I love your mum. And you're important to me too. I know I'm not your dad, but I'm hoping we can form that kind of relationship."

"I miss him."

I squeeze his shoulder. "I know you do. And I bet anything that you all wish he were here right now. But you're stuck with me, so we have to make the most of it. Okay?"

His smile is small, but I'll take it as a win. "Okay."

He sighs, and I pull him closer. "You can lean on me. I hope you know that. I'm here for anything you need."

"I just wish Mum would come back."

"Me too. But we just have to be patient and give her time. Braden's in the best place he could be."

"Hunter?"

I look up. "Gary? What are you doing here?"

Xander nudges my arm. "That's the guy who did CPR on Braden."

"What?"

Gary's lips twitch. "That boy. Is he okay? There wasn't anything I could do for the other one, but ..."

"You saved Braden?" My heart thuds.

He cradles the back of his neck. "I nearly broke my sobriety tonight. That's where I was going when I saw the accident. And that First Aid refresher really helped."

"Thank you. You could have saved my boy's life."

"Your boy?" Gary asks.

I look at Xander. "My boy."

Xander's eyes fill with emotion and he flings his arms around me. This is it. This is the emotional connection he needed for my relationship with his mother to be okay.

I wrap my arms around him, and do what I hope a father would—give him the comfort he needs.

"I ... I don't know what to say." Gary stands there, his eyes wide.

"Thank you so much. His mother and I are so grateful."

I don't care what it takes to help this guy out. I'll do anything after what he's done.

"Is he going to be okay?"

I swallow hard. "I'm not sure. His mum is with him now, and we're waiting to hear."

"Can I sit with you?"

I gesture toward the seat. "Sure."

He takes a seat a short distance from me, but I close my eyes and focus on Xander beside me.

I'm here for them, Scott. I always will be.

"MR EMERSON? Mrs Cooper asked for you and Xander."

The nurse stands in front of us, and I look up.

"Thank you."

Xander and I rise from our seats, and he takes a deep breath.

"Come on, mate. Let's go and see your brother."

I turn to Gary. "I'll text you. Go home and get some rest."

He nods. "Please. I'd like to make sure the boy's going to be okay."

"Sure thing." I reach down and grip his shoulder before turning back.

We follow the nurse down the corridor until we reach a room. She opens the door for us, and I follow Xander through, nearly stopping in my tracks when I see Braden lying motionless in his hospital bed, Chloe's hand clamped around his.

It breaks my heart, but the ECG machine beeps rhythmically beside them, and I'm more than grateful to hear the sound.

"Chloe," I whisper.

She looks up and smiles. "Hey."

"Mum?" Xander steps forward. "Is he okay?"

Chloe nods. "He has to have surgery shortly to relieve some pressure, and they think he'll be fine. But we have to see what happens when he wakes up."

"Are you okay?" My eyes are on her as Xander makes his way to the other side of the bed. I walk over to Chloe and grip her shoulder.

"No." She leans her head on my hand. "But I'm better now you and Xander are here. Braden needs all of us."

"I'm sorry."

The nurse opens the door, and I move to hold it while she brings in two more chairs.

"Let me know if you need anything else," she says.

"Thank you."

She leaves us, and I hand one chair to Xander on the other side of the bed before carrying mine to sit next to Chloe.

"I guess our secret's out." She leans against me, and I kiss her temple.

"Xander and I talked about it in the waiting room. We're cool."

She pulls back, her eyes searching mine. "I'm glad. We need to talk."

I take her hand in mine and squeeze. "We do. But that can wait for now."

Her lower lip wobbles, and I press my forehead to hers. "When this is over and Braden's back home, we'll work it all out, Chlo."

"I hope so."

When I pull back, tears spill down her cheeks. I'd move heaven and earth to stop her from going through this, and I pull her into my arms and just hold her while she cries.

"Mum?" Xander rounds the bed.

She raises her head to look at him. "I'm okay. Just scared."

"I'm sorry we lied to you. You seem like you've had a lot on your mind, and we didn't want to worry you more."

Chloe turns and brushes his hair off his face. "I always worry. We'll talk about this later, but right now we need to focus on your brother. I'm so glad you're okay."

He leans over and hugs her. "I'm just really sorry."

"I know, sweetheart."

The door opens, and the nurse enters "It's time for us to take Braden for his surgery. You're welcome to stay in here or wait in the waiting room. There's a kitchen just down the corridor to your left with coffee and tea if you need it."

I force a small smile. "Appreciate it."

Two more nurses appear and we all move back to give them space to work, and then we're left in an empty room and all there is to do is wait.

But we'll wait as a family, because that's what we are now.

TWENTY-NINE

CHLOE

I NEVER GOT the chance to say goodbye to Scott.

I kissed him before he went to work that morning, and that's the last time I ever saw him.

My relief when they wheeled Braden back into the room alive was overwhelming. And now he's lying in the hospital bed, and I feel so useless.

My heart is in my throat as his chest rises and falls while we wait for him to wake up. It takes me back to when he was born, a little early, and the smaller of the two boys. Xander was younger by three minutes, and louder.

Braden was always the quiet, gentler one.

I don't know what I'll do if I lose him. It doesn't bear thinking about. But the thought nags at me the whole time I watch over him.

"Coffee."

I look up to see Hunter standing over me with a cupholder, and a couple of paper bags in his other hand. Xander arrives right behind him with his own drink and food.

"Thank you."

He hands me a takeaway cup, and I take a sip and smile.

"Caramel syrup?"

"Xander tipped me off that you had a sweet tooth now. I guess there's still a lot we have to learn about each other."

I take another sip. "Sometimes. I have to be in the mood for it, but this is a good time."

He holds up the bags. "I also got a sweet pastry and a savoury one for you to choose from. You need to eat."

"The savoury one would be nice. I appreciate you taking care of me."

Hunter leans over and presses a kiss to my forehead. "Taking care of you is my job now."

I smile. "You're so good at it."

Across the room, Xander makes a sound that resembles a cat coughing up a fur ball.

"You know, when I said we were okay with you two, that didn't mean you had to do *that* in front of us."

"Do what?" Hunter laughs.

"That lovey-dovey shit."

"You're going to have to get used to it."

Xander rolls his eyes. "It's not fair."

I laugh, placing my hand on Hunter's chest. "All we need now is for Braden to wake up and we'll all be happy."

"I'm going out to get some fresh air and give you two some alone time." Xander stands, tosses his empty chip packet into the bin, and leaves the room.

I stare at the door momentarily as it closes behind him, my heart swelling at his teenage chivalry.

"Do you think he's okay?" Hunter asks.

"He'll be fine as long as Braden is."

"M ... Mum?" Braden's voice is croaky, but it's the sweetest sound I've ever heard in my life.

I push myself out of the chair and stand beside the bed. "I'm here."

"What happened?"

"You were in an accident, and you got a head injury. The doctor operated to relieve pressure, and we've been waiting for you to wake up."

"Xander!" The ECG beeps quicker as Braden tries to sit up, his breathing elevated. "Is ... is Xander okay?"

I lay my palm on his chest and gently coax him back down. "He's fine. He just stepped out to get some fresh air.

He closes his eyes for a second and sucks in a few deep breaths. "What about Lincoln?"

I swallow hard.

"Mum? What happened to Lincoln?"

I bite my bottom lip. "He didn't make it."

"What?"

"Honey, Lincoln died. I'm so sorry."

Braden tears up. I lean over and wrap my arms around him while he cries on my shoulder.

The door opens. "I was halfway out, and I had a feeling I should ... Braden!" Hope floods Xander's expression, and he walks toward the bed. Hunter meets him part way and offers him his arms.

I have tears of my own as the man I love becomes my child's father in that moment.

He loves all of us.

He was right. I had to find myself before we became a family, but as of this moment, that's what we are.

"Don't be angry with us, Mum. Please," Braden whispers.

"I'm not going to pretend I'm happy about you not calling me instead of getting in that car, but given that I could have lost both of you, I don't even know what to do as far as punishment goes. I'll just be glad to have you home." I kiss his cheek.

"All I could think about was this is how Dad died," Xander says. "What do we do now?"

"Braden gets better and comes home, and we move on with our lives. I'll get you both those driving lessons you want and we'll do this properly."

"I can teach them to drive," Hunter says.

He looks at me with so much love, even Braden's eyes widen as he looks between us.

"Mum and Hunter are together," Xander says.

Braden's whole face lights up. "Awesome."

"You're happy about it?"

He nods. "I already told you I approve."

"You did?" Hunter asks.

"After you took care of Mum that night ..." His eyes widen again. "Eww."

Hunter laughs. "Nothing happened that night."

"Good because eww."

I laugh, rolling my eyes at my son.

Everything's as it should be.

THIRTY
HUNTER

IT'S BEEN A LONG NIGHT.

I haven't paid much attention to the time, but lunch being brought in for Braden is a sign that we've been here all night.

Chloe looks dead on her feet, and Xander's no different.

"Why don't we go home and let Braden get some sleep?" I say.

Braden smiles. "Promise?"

"I don't know ..." Chloe starts.

"I'll carry you out of here if I have to."

Braden cocks an eyebrow. "Please. No foreplay in my hospital room."

"Eww." Xander laughs.

"I just want to make sure your mother gets a good sleep. She needs it."

Braden nods. "You do have bags under your eyes, Mum."

"Thanks." Chloe laughs.

"Seriously, Mum, go. Come back tomorrow."

Xander takes a step forward. "I found your phone beside the car. The screen's smashed, but it's still working."

Xander hands Braden his phone.

Braden groans. "Mum ..."

"We'll get it fixed when you get out of hospital. In the meantime, have a good sleep." Chloe leans over to press a kiss to his forehead.

"By the way. I've been texting that girl you like. She's really keen to nurse you back to health." Xander waggles his eyebrows.

"You what?" Braden's expression drops.

"She sent you a text about an hour ago, so I replied. Sounds like word has spread about the crash."

I look at Chloe. "Do they often pretend to be one another?"

She shakes her head and laughs. "They haven't for a long time."

"Thank God for that because I'm pretty sure I know which is which, but I don't think it'd take too much to fool me."

"We wouldn't do that to you, Hunter," Xander says, exchanging a grin with his brother.

"Whatever." I ruffle his hair.

Chloe tugs on my sleeve and I turn to see the look of utter adoration written all over her face. "Let's go home."

Home.

I'll need to swing by Scott's grave sometime and apologise for moving into his dream home, because that's what I plan to do, but I'm not going to apologise for loving Chloe.

I'd still love to see him once more and renew our friendship. Instead, I'll make sure his family becomes mine and I'll take care of them all.

"See you tomorrow, Braden. Good luck with the girl," I say.

He looks up, a dazed expression on his face. "She likes me."

Chloe's eyes widen.

"Let's just deal with this tomorrow." I grab Chloe's hand. "Catch you later, Braden. I'm glad you're okay."

"Thanks, Hunter."

He catches me off guard, flashing a smile that looks so much like his dad it hits me square in the chest.

"Anyway, we are going to let you have some sleep," Chloe says.

It's the weirdest feeling as we walk out, and I catch one last glimpse of Braden before we're out in the corridor.

I'm just so relieved he's safe.

Xander walks a little ahead of us, while I loop my arm around Chloe's waist and we make our way out of the hospital and toward the car.

"Thank you for staying with us," she says.

"There's nowhere else I want to be." I lean over and press a kiss into her hair.

The cool breeze that greets us outside is refreshing after being inside the hospital for so long, and I take a deep breath.

Chloe leans against me for support. She must be exhausted.

"I'll pay for the parking," she says.

"I've got it. Just get in the car."

She shakes her head and smiles. "You're so bossy."

"You should be used to it by now."

I peck her on the lips while Xander rolls his eyes again. Turning toward him, I throw him the car keys and point.

"The car's right over there. Go and unlock it, and I'll be there in a minute."

He grumbles something about PDAs.

Chloe furrows her brow. "What's a PDA?"

He rolls his eyes as if his mother belongs with the dinosaurs. "Public Display of Affection."

"Oh." She laughs.

I shake my head and stick my credit card in the machine to pay.

It's time to go home.

CHLOE LETS out a big sigh as we walk into the kitchen.

It must be a relief to be home, even though Braden's still back in the hospital. But in a few days, he'll be able to join us, and I'm sure she'll feel whole again.

"Take a seat, Chlo. I'll cook something up for us."

"Can we make steak and potatoes like you did that other time?" Xander asks.

I smile. He's nowhere near as dark and sulky as he was when we first met. I hope this means he really has accepted my relationship with his mother. "Sure thing. Want to help?"

He nods.

"Get the steak out of the freezer while I make sure your mum's off her feet."

I follow her into the living room and peek over my shoulder to make sure Xander can't see.

"I can find my way to the couch myself," Chloe says.

Reaching for her arm, I turn her to face me.

Her eyes widen. "Hunter—"

I claim her mouth, tasting her coconut lip gloss and losing myself as I wrap my arms around her waist. She laughs against my lips, and I let go of a sigh when I let her up for air.

"I've missed that."

"You must have. I haven't brushed my teeth since yesterday morning." She grins.

"You still taste like you."

Chloe reaches up to stroke my beard. "I've missed you."

"I haven't forgotten what you told me in the car. It's been kind of hard not to address it." I look down at her stomach. "I'm guessing the boys don't know yet?"

She shakes her head. "No one does. And I'm so sorry to tell you that way."

"Don't apologise. It doesn't mean anything less 'cause of the way you told me."

Her tired smile warms my heart.

"I hope you're okay with it."

"Okay with it? That's a question I should be asking you seeing as we weren't together when you found out."

She shrugs. "The timing could have been better, but I did always want more children."

"Then there's nothing more to talk about." I reach for her hands and entwine our fingers. "As long as you really are ready for this."

"It's all I want."

I kiss her again. "Me too. Take a seat and I'll bring you some food when it's ready."

She flops on the couch and closes her eyes.

It takes a moment for me to turn around because all I want to do is look at her. This wasn't how I saw our reunion happen, but this is it. I'll feel better when Braden's home, but this is my family now.

"Hunter," Xander calls. "I just put the steak in the microwave to defrost."

I grimace. Not my favourite way to do things, but he's hungry. And, as if on cue, my stomach rumbles.

"Okay, kid, let's get this done. Want to peel the potatoes? I'll find the garlic and onions to go with them."

We work quietly and quickly, side by side. Xander's good at following instructions, and before long the kitchen's full of the scent and sizzles of the food cooking.

He's so much like his dad, but once he opens up it's a sight to behold.

"Look at this." Chloe walks up behind me and grips my shoulder.

I shake the frying pan. "We're nearly done. Hope you're hungry. I think Xander's plan was to feed an army."

"I'm starved," Xander says.

"You'll have to do this again when Braden's home. He'll be annoyed at missing out." Chloe presses a kiss to my bicep before sitting at the table. "But it makes me happy to see the two of you working together."

Xander and I fill three plates and he places some food in front of his mother before sitting beside her. I sit on the other side.

Before I even have time to catch my breath, he starts shovelling the potatoes into his mouth. "These are so good."

"Well, now you know how to make them too, so you can cook for us."

He grins. "Sounds good."

I look over at Chloe. Sure enough, she's picking at her plate. "What about you?"

"It's really lovely. I'm just tired."

"Eat up and then we can go and get some sleep."

"Grandma would say you should eat more, Mum. You're too thin." Xander does what seems to be an impression of Chloe's mother.

Chloe laughs. "Point taken."

"At least this is edible." He shrugs.

Chloe forks a piece of meat and potato and takes a big bite.

Xander shoots a smile at me before hoovering up what's left on his plate. "That was so good. You can cook for us any time," he says.

"I'm thinking it'll have to be a fairly regular thing." I meet Chloe's gaze. There's no going back now whatever happens.

I know she loves me.

After we've finished eating, Xander collects our plates and loads up the dishwasher without being asked. I almost feel like the intruder, Chloe's kids are so dedicated to her. But they've been through so much, and them letting me into their world can only grow from here.

"I'm going to bed. If anything happens with Braden ..."

"I'll come and wake you up." Chloe smiles at him.

He bends over and kisses her cheek. "Have a good sleep, Mum."

"You too, sweetheart."

She turns and watches him leave before standing.

I stand beside her and take her hand in mine. "Are you okay?"

"What if this girl turns out to be serious with Braden? I don't want my babies having sex. I don't even want to think about it."

I chuckle and bury my face in her neck. "I'm not sure you get a say in it. We'll just make sure they're both safe."

"They've already had the talk with me." She pulls away and turns her head. "I'm glad you're here though. I doubt they'll want to go into any detail with their mother."

"I'll do my best."

"I know you will. Thank you for loving them."

"It's easy when they're a part of two people I love."

Chloe swallows hard. "Should we go and lie down now?"

"Only a lie down?"

She laughs. "I'm way too tired for anything else."

I shrug. "It was worth a try."

She leans against me as we walk up the stairs together, and I slip an arm around her waist.

Reaching her bedroom door, she slides her arms around my neck.

"Stay the night with us?"

"Are you ready for that?"

She leans into me and closes her eyes. "I don't want to waste another minute of my life without you."

I wrap my arms around her and press a kiss to her forehead. "I love you."

She sniffs. "I'm sorry I kept you waiting."

"It doesn't matter now. All that matters is that we're together and the boys are safe."

"They're never leaving this house again."

I chuckle. "We'll talk about it later. I'm not sure either of them will want to go anywhere for a while."

"I could have lost both of them." She clings a little tighter.

"But you didn't, and they're both okay. We just need to get Braden home and we can all start this new life. And get ready for our little one to arrive." I kiss her again. "Let's get to bed."

"I bought a new bed."

"You did?"

She leans back and gives me a small smile. "My old one's in the spare room. I couldn't quite bring myself to get rid of it, but I have a nice new comfortable one."

"With plenty of room for me?"

"I bought it with you in mind." Her smile widens. "It's plenty big."

She pushes open the door.

The room's different. Not in decor, but the bed and the other furniture don't look like they used to.

"It's all new. I wanted a fresh start."

"Looks good. Plenty of room for my stuff."

Chloe turns to look at me. "Is that you deciding to move into my house?"

I shrug. "You've made this place your own. Besides, there's more space here."

She rubs her neck before pulling her T-shirt over her head.

"Want a neck rub?"

"I'll be fine. That chair was okay, but nothing like sleeping in your own bed."

I laugh as she pulls my shirt on. "You kept it?"

"I've been sleeping in it. It made me think of you."

I tug off the shirt I'm wearing and drop my pants to the floor while she climbs into bed. She sighs contentedly as I slide in beside her and pull her into my arms. It feels like forever since we've been like this, and after tonight I have no intention to spend another night without her.

"You give the best hugs." She places a palm on my chest.

"Glad you like them."

"I've missed them. I've missed you."

I cup her cheek. "I need to tell you about Piper."

Chloe's expression tightens. Her eyes search mine.

"Nothing happened. She turned up because she heard we'd been spending time together and she wanted to stick her nose in. Then she left. I should have said something that day, and I didn't, and I feel bad for not doing anything."

She blinks rapidly. "I thought maybe you got sick of waiting."

"I would have waited forever for you. You're the only one I want."

Tears fill her eyes. "Hunter."

"Let it all out, sweetheart. You're safe here with me. And you always will be."

Her warm tears spill onto my chest, and I close my eyes and hold her tight. How frightened she must have been to get that call when she's already been through so much.

I can't promise her that nothing will ever happen to me, but I can be the man she needs me to be.

"I've got you, Chloe. Always."

Wiping her cheeks with my thumb, I take in the sight of her. I'm so in love with her that watching her takes my breath away. After pushing her blonde hair off her face, I run a finger over the freckles on her nose.

"What are you doing?"

"Touching you."

Her lips twitch as I run my finger down her throat and over her breasts. "It's hard to believe there's anything in there." I place my hand on her stomach.

She laughs. "You'll see it soon enough. I looked like I'd swallowed a beach ball with the twins."

I raise my eyebrows. "What if it's twins?"

She lets out a sigh. "We'll cross that bridge if we come to it."

"You know I wouldn't mind either way."

Chloe plants a kiss on my chest. "Whatever will be, will be. What about gender? Any preference?"

"I'm happy whatever we have."

"Me too. I always thought it'd be nice to have a girl after two boys, but either way is good."

I tap her cheek. "If we have a girl, I hope she gets your freckles."

Chloe screws up her nose. "No way."

"I always thought they were cute. I'm glad you don't cover them up."

Compliments still bring a blush to her cheeks, and I love seeing her like this. She's obviously got Braden on her mind, but whatever distraction I can bring to the conversation, I will.

He's safe and will hopefully be home in the next few days.

And then we can all start life as a family together.

THIRTY-ONE
CHLOE

TWO WEEKS LATER, there's one more thing I need to do before I move ahead.

I could leave things as they are, but I can either continue to put up with Kay's negativity or I can make the choice to cut her out of my life.

She can have a relationship with her grandchildren without me if that's what she wants. But I won't put up with her trying to make me feel as if I love Scott less by moving on with my life.

It's time to stand up to her.

I called earlier to let her know I'd be coming, but now I'm in her driveway and tension pools in my stomach.

But there's no backing down from this.

Taking a deep breath, I get out of the car and walk toward the house. The back door's open, and I give it a quick tap.

"Kay? It's Chloe."

She appears from the other end of the kitchen. "Come in. Are the boys with you?"

"No. It's just me today."

I kick off my shoes on the doorstep and walk into the house.

"Coffee?"

"That would be lovely."

Her smile shows me she's unsure of why I'm here, and I'm not about to lay it out until we're both sitting down and she's calm. I'm sure she won't be happy, but which way she'll go, I don't know.

"Take a seat in the living room, and I'll bring it through."

"Thank you."

I take a deep breath as I walk into the room. This house is so full of memories, and I walk to the shelves on the wall and pick up a photo of Scott. It was taken just before we left for Auckland. Running my finger down the glass, I smile.

"He was so handsome," Kay says. "That floppy hair and those dimples. The boys inherited those."

I put the photo back down. "They inherited a lot from him."

She hands me my coffee and we sit on the couch together.

I take a sip. "That's so good."

"You said you had to talk to me?"

Placing the coffee cup on the table, I wait as she does the same before I speak.

"There's something I need to tell you, Kay. I know you're not going to like it, but I'm not going to put up with your negativity anymore."

She clamps her lips together, and I'm thankful because I'm not sure how I'd handle her biting back.

"I'm in love with Hunter Emerson. We're having a baby."

Her lower lip wobbles. "Is that why you buried Scott?"

I shake my head. "No. We came home for that, but realising I could have a new life gave me the strength to do it."

Tears fill her eyes.

"I loved Scott with all my heart. We grew up together, got through all the tough things together, and we were devoted to each other until the day he died. For four years, my heart's been so heavy because he's not with me, and I'd still give anything for him to come back."

She swallows hard, opens her mouth, and then closes it again. I know this is hard for her. Scott was her only son. But I'm a grown up who has to make my own decisions now.

I choose my life.

"I never planned to fall for Hunter. But he loves me, and he loves my boys, and he respects Scott's legacy. I couldn't love anyone who didn't do that. He gave me time and space to work this all out for myself. And I love him, Kay, just as I still love Scott."

Tears spill down her cheeks, and she gives me a short, sharp nod. "All I wanted was to make sure Scott's boys were taken care of."

"I'm their mother. I've put them first all their lives. I always will. Hunter was Scott's best friend, and he'll be there for our boys no matter what. I have faith in that."

For seventeen years, our relationship has been toxic. And I'm glad I'm getting this out in the open. It should have been done years ago instead of this passive aggressive game.

"I miss Scott," she says.

"So do I." Tears prick my eyes. "He never failed to tell me he loved me. Every single day. I've got this hole in my heart that'll never mend."

"And Hunter loves you like that too?"

I nod. "He was unexpected, but yes, he loves me like that too."

She reaches for my hand. "I'm glad. Will you still bring the boys to see me?"

I place my other hand on hers. "Of course. You'll always be their grandmother."

"And your little one?" She sniffs. "You know I don't like to gossip, but I don't think Hunter has much of a relationship with his parents. I could ..."

"You're family. You're always welcome."

Her lips spread into a cautious smile. "Thank you, Chloe. I know I was hard on you, but I just loved Scott so much."

"I know."

"I hope you're happy. It's what you all deserve. And there's a part of me that's glad it's Hunter. He won't drag you around the world."

I shake my head. "We're staying right here."

"And having a baby. I always hoped you and Scott would have more. This is wonderful."

My smile grows. "It's not something I thought I'd be doing with someone new, but I'm very happy. Hunter's over the moon. I don't think he can quite believe it."

"He doesn't have children, does he?"

I shake my head. "No. This is his first."

"He's a good man, Chloe."

"He really is. He'll be a good father to all my children."

There's a moment when she takes in what I said as it registers on her face and her mouth opens and closes.

"Scott will always be Braden and Xander's father, but now they'll have two dads. Hunter doesn't want to try and replace Scott, but he will be there for them when they need him. He loves them."

She picks up her coffee and takes a sip. "Then, I'm happy for you. I just wish Scott was here."

"Me too."

THE SCENT of onion and garlic floats through the air as I walk into the kitchen, and my mouth waters.

Hunter stands at the cooktop making lunch. He looks up at me and smiles as I walk through the door.

"Give me one second." Flicking off the element, he turns toward me. "I was just about to put yours in the fridge."

"What is it?"

"I cooked up some of those potatoes the boys like."

I laugh. "They so have you twisted around their little fingers."

He shrugs. "I don't mind."

"Just wait until the baby arrives. You're so screwed."

Hunter wraps his arms around my waist. "Where have you been?"

"I went to see Scott's mother."

"Oh."

I sigh. "It's long overdue. But I think we've come to some peace. She's very excited about our baby too."

He chuckles, kissing the top of my head. "Not as excited as I am."

"I don't think anyone's as excited as you." I raise my face, and he gives me a tender kiss on the lips.

"Where are the boys?" I ask.

"Braden's in his room playing games and Xander's gone to rugby practice."

I facepalm. "I forgot his rugby practice."

"It's okay. I sorted it. But I have to pick him up in about an hour." A slow smile spreads across his lips. "So, I figure, I have about an hour."

"An hour for what?"

He raises his hand to my face, running his thumb down my cheek. "Well, you're already pregnant, but we could practice what got you in that state."

I laugh. "That sounds interesting."

"I love you, Chloe," he says.

And then he scoops me into his arms and I laugh silently against his shoulder as he carries me up the stairs, past Braden's closed door and into our bedroom.

Life couldn't be better.

THIRTY-TWO

CHLOE

"CHLOE."

I turn at the sound of Dad's voice behind me. His face is full of joy with a smile that extends from his lips up to his eyes.

"You look beautiful," he says, crossing the room, his arms open.

"Bit different to jeans and a registry office." I laugh, but I wanted this day to be as different to my last wedding day as possible.

"Very different. You looked beautiful for that day too, if I didn't say it back then." He has tears in his eyes, and I reach up and wipe them away

Hunter and I decided to marry before the baby arrived, and then he organised this day in record time. Anyone would think he was anxious. We haven't yet reached twelve weeks, so the only people we've told about the baby are Braden and Xander.

I run my hand down the front of my pale yellow dress and touch the tiny bump that's recently appeared.

"Thanks, Dad." I lean forward and peck him on the cheek.

"Hunter's a lucky man. But I might be biased." He winks at me, and I grasp his arm, leaning into him.

"Love you."

"I love you too. Let's get you married."

I loop my arm into his and take a deep breath. I never thought I'd have a second wedding day, yet here I am about to marry my best friend. He gets me on a level no one else does, and he loves our family so much.

Coming home was the best choice I ever made.

Dad leads me out the back door, past the pool and onto the lawn where Hunter waits. Braden and Xander stand at his side, and I tear up when I lay eyes on all three of my boys standing together.

Hunter shines so bright as he meets my gaze. His whole handsome face lights up, and I take a deep breath as we approach.

It's a small gathering. My parents, Caleb, Darren and Meredith with their children, Kay and Preston. Hunter's relationship with his parents is still fractured, and he wanted today to be without tension, so they weren't invited. I didn't push him—it's only because Kay's made such an effort with me since the day we talked it out that she's here.

Hunter steps forward as we approach, and takes my hand in his as my father drops his arm.

"She's all yours," Dad says.

I meet Hunter's gaze and all I see is love. "Thank you," Hunter says.

He squeezes my hand as we turn to the celebrant.

But I barely pay any attention as she speaks until it comes up to the part where we exchange vows.

And then Hunter takes my other hand as we face one another.

"Chloe. You've brought the light to my life where there was none. And you gave me the family I always wanted. I'm a man of few words, but just know that I'll always love and cherish you, and I'll never take what we have for granted."

My eyes swim with tears, and I let them fall, not worrying about wiping them away.

"Chloe?" The celebrant says.

I draw in a breath. "Hunter. You gave me a second chance for love when I didn't think that was even possible. I'm just looking forward to spending the rest of my life with you."

Hunter and I gaze at each other. There was a time in my life when I never thought I'd be happy again, but he changed all that for me.

And I'll spend my days showing him just how much.

THIRTY-THREE
HUNTER

I'VE NEVER BEEN SO scared in my whole life.

Chloe hasn't given birth in seventeen years, but she's like a pro, trying her best to calm me. But watching the pain she's in isn't easy.

I'd give anything to take it all away.

She places her hands on her lower back and straightens up. Her eyes are closed, and she breaths in through her nose and out through her mouth.

I hold her hand, I fetch her water, but otherwise I feel useless.

And somehow in between contractions, she smiles and I fall in love with her all over again.

"Are you okay?" she asks.

I laugh. "I'll be fine. I just worry about you."

She shrugs. "It sucks, but it'll be over soon. Kidney stones were worse."

"Did it take this long with the boys?"

Chloe laughs before grimacing and gripping the back of my chair. "This'll be a lot faster, I think."

"How's it going?" The midwife walks back in. She left us to it while Chloe's labour progressed, but I've noticed her visits are more frequent.

Chloe nods. "The contractions are definitely stronger. And faster."

"Let's have a look at you."

I hold Chloe's arm as she climbs up onto the bed.

She strokes my cheek. "Don't look so worried, Hunter. It'll be over soon."

"I'm allowed to worry about my wife."

"Well, you won't have much longer to go. Chloe, you're at nine centimetres. One more and it'll be time to push."

Chloe leans against me.

"Want some help getting up?"

She shakes her head. "I think I'll stay here for now."

For a moment, I just sit and hold her hand. She screws up her face, and I see the next contraction coming.

"How are we doing, Chloe?" the midwife says.

"I really want to push. Does that make sense?"

She smiles. "Nothing really makes sense about giving birth. Let's take another look."

Her brows rise. "This baby's ready to come. Next contraction, push."

"You ready for this, Mr Emerson?" Chloe asks.

I grin. "I should ask you that, Mrs Emerson."

I lean over and kiss her, and her grip tightens as the next contraction hits. I'm not even sure how long it takes, but my woman is a machine.

My heart pounds at the sight of the baby's head.

My own head's so light I feel like I'm going to faint. I take deep breaths right along with Chloe as she pushes.

The rest of our daughter slides out of Chloe's body. She's small, wrinkled, and messy. But I love her the moment I set eyes on her.

It's the grossest and most beautiful thing I think I've ever seen in my life.

Chloe's a goddess. She lays back, red faced and covered in sweat, but I've never loved her so much. She's made my dreams come true.

I lean over and wrap my arms around her shoulders, kissing her lips.

"We did it," she whispers.

"You did. I just watched." I chuckle, leaning my forehead on hers.

"Would you like to cut the cord?" The midwife asks.

I turn my head. "Please."

She hands me the scissors and shows me where to make the cut. I'm not even sure I'll remember any of this as waves of love wash over me.

It all happens so fast as our little girl is placed on Chloe's chest, her ear resting on Chloe's heart, listening to it beat.

There's a lump in my throat so big I don't know if I'll ever be able to swallow again.

"She has your eyes," Chloe says.

"Do you think so?" I croak.

"They could change, but both the boys had blue eyes. Hers are so dark. I hope they don't change."

"Me too."

"You can touch her."

I meet Chloe's gaze. "She's so small."

"She needs to get to know her daddy."

My hand shakes as I reach out and touch her back. Her skin's all fuzzy, and my heart leaps as I feel her take a breath.

"You're more gentle than you think you are, Hunter. You won't hurt her."

"Is it that obvious?" I laugh.

"You're scared of a baby. I'm sure that's pretty common." Chloe's tone is soft.

"I'm not scared."

"She won't break." Chloe leans her head on my arm. "Talk to her. She's heard your voice for months, she'll be used to it."

"Hey, little one." I'm still not sure how to process all this. It's all so much.

Her little mouth purses and I'm lost.

She's perfect.

AFTER SHE'S CLOTHED and fed, Chloe rocks our daughter in her arms while I take photos.

So many photos.

"It's Daddy's turn to give you a cuddle," she coos.

I drop my phone on the bedside cabinet and swallow hard. Tears prick my eyes at the thought of holding my daughter.

Her tiny face screws up and Chloe laughs. "It's okay, sweet girl. Your father's going to take good care of you."

Tears roll down my cheeks as the little bundle is placed in my arms.

My daughter looks up at me, her unfocused dark eyes staring.

"Are you real?" I whisper.

All my adult life, I wanted a family. I thought any chance of that was long gone with my divorce. I thought I was too old to make a fresh start.

Chloe proved all of that wrong.

I look at Chloe through teary eyes, and she seems to be tearing up herself.

"She's real. Look what we made."

"Thank you," I croak.

Chloe reaches over and brushes away my tears. "You deserve it all, big guy."

"I love you."

"I love you too." She draws a circle on our baby girl's nose with the tip of her finger. "And your brothers will love you," she says with a light tap. Chloe looks at the clock above the door to her room. "But visiting hours have closed, so they'll have to wait until morning to meet their little sister."

"Their little sister." I chuckle. "I bet they never thought this day would come either."

"Nope, but they'll be good big brothers." She strokes the top of our daughter's head. "She'll always be loved and protected, and she'll have her father with her the whole way."

I sniff. "She will."

"And I know she's just been born, but I'd like one more. Braden and Xander always had each other when they were growing up, and I don't want her to be by herself."

Grinning, I lean over to kiss her. "I'll make as many babies with you as you want."

She smiles. "Just one more. Before I get too old to make them."

"I don't know what to say to that without getting myself in trouble."

Chloe laughs. "It's okay. I'd also like to get it out of the way so we get a chance to live some of our lives just the two of us after they all leave home."

I gape at her. "My girl's *never* leaving home."

"They all do one day. We just have to make the most of them before they do."

Her eyes are so tired, and all I want to do is take the two of them home and care for them. But it's late, and the earliest we'll go home is tomorrow.

There's no way I'm leaving the hospital tonight.

I nestle into the comfy chair in the corner, our baby in my arms.

"What should we call her?"

Chloe smiles. "You choose."

"Really? I thought we were doing this together." I look back at my baby girl. We spent hours discussing names but never coming to any resolution.

"I named Braden and Xander. I think you can name our babies." Her hazy eyes are full of love. I could live in this moment forever.

"My favourite name is Chloe. I'm not sure that's going to work."

She laughs, leaning against her pillow. "You goofball."

"How about Hannah?"

Chloe smiles. "Your grandmother's name."

"You remember." God how I love this woman. My grandmother died when I was thirteen, and she was the last grandparent I had. We've not really discussed her recently. She's remembered from when we were kids.

"I know everything about you, Hunter Emerson. Don't you ever forget." Her lips quirk.

"It's impossible to."

"I like Hannah. It's beautiful," she says.

I lean back. "It suits her. Try and get some sleep. Hopefully I can take you two home in the morning."

"Hope so."

That's the last thing she says before she dozes. I doubt Chloe's fully asleep as I don't know if I could sleep in the hospital. But I sit in the quiet and hold my daughter on one of the best days of my life.

It's with great reluctance that I surrender her to the crib in order to return to the chair to grab some sleep myself.

Not that I'll sleep well.

Instead, I watch Chloe. What she went through today was insane, and all to give life to that little girl. It just makes me love her even more.

"I THOUGHT we'd never get out of there." Chloe puffs to blow a stray hair out of her face.

It's close to midday, but we're on our way home after an up and down night in the hospital. Hannah likes her food, and she's got a good set of lungs on her.

I smile to myself at the thought of the twins dealing with that.

"Hunter?"

"Sorry?" I shoot a glance at Chloe. We left the hospital about five minutes ago, and I think we're both looking forward to sleeping in our own bed tonight. Not that I think Hannah will let us get much sleep.

"Are you okay?"

Her cheeks are still flushed, and she looks so refreshed compared to how I feel.

"Me? I'm fine. How about you?"

"I'll just be glad to get home. You looked a million miles away."

I smile. "Just thinking about how much the boys will love their sister. Until she screams."

"They'll just have to deal with it. At least there aren't two screaming babies this time."

"Thank heavens for small mercies."

Chloe closes her eyes, and I smile.

It wouldn't matter to me if there were. I'd still be the happiest man alive right now. And I can't wait to get home for us all to be together.

When I think back to what life was like before Chloe returned, I wonder how I got through the day. Now, our days are filled with love and laughter, and my family is all I could ever have wished for.

It's not a long drive, and as I draw the car to a stop in the driveway, Chloe jerks awake.

"Sorry." I take her hand and squeeze it.

"Don't apologise. I'm just going to grab a nap where I can." Her sleepy smile shows just how tired she is.

"Let's go and see the boys." I lean over and peck her on the lips.

Stepping out of the car, I open the back door and grab Chloe's bag. I raise the handle of the baby capsule until it clicks into place, and lift it out of the back seat.

"I'll take it." Chloe reaches for the car seat.

"I've got it. Get inside and put your feet up."

Her tired eyes are so full of love. "You're so good to me."

"You did all the hard work. Now I get to pamper you."

Chloe kisses my cheek. "Sounds good to me."

I follow her into the house, and as we walk through the door, the boys come bounding down the stairs.

"Where is she?" Braden pushes Xander out of the way.

"Hey." Xander pushes him back.

"You two have to settle down before I let you anywhere near her."

Reaching the kitchen, I place the baby capsule on the table. "Here's your sister."

"She's tiny," Braden says.

"She's bigger than either of you were." Chloe comes up behind me, sliding one arm around my waist. I plant a kiss on her temple.

"She's beautiful." Xander's eyes shine with happiness. This is one proud big brother. No matter what happens, I know he'll always be there for Hannah. "Did you name her?"

"Hannah. It was my grandmother's name."

He nods. "Cool."

I grip his shoulder. "She's gonna be nuts about you when she gets bigger. Both of you."

His smile is magical. "I always wanted a sister."

Chloe's grip tightens around me.

"Me too," Braden says. "Beats having a brother."

Xander shoots a glare at Braden, and I suppress a smile, turning back to Chloe. She's still a little pale, and she'll need more sleep, but I'll be right here to give her all the support she needs.

She just gave me the world.

It's the least I can do in return.

LEAVING the boys to clean up after lunch, I follow Chloe upstairs with the baby to get some rest.

For a while, Hannah's sleeping in our room right beside the bed, and the sight of Chloe lowering Hannah into her bassinet makes me smile.

I love my life.

"I've been looking forward to sleeping in my own bed all day," Chloe says.

"I'm just looking forward to sleep."

She laughs. "That might be hard to come by for a while."

I look down at our daughter, sleeping peacefully. It won't last long, but right now she's content.

"She's worth it."

Chloe pats my chest and undresses, pulling one of my shirts over her head. It's the one she took the first night we were together, and I wrote it off a long time ago.

It doesn't matter.

She climbs into our bed and closes her eyes.

For a moment, I just watch her.

Undressing, I slip into bed beside Chloe and slide my arms around her. She snuggles in tight and smiles.

"You always give the best hugs."

"I love holding you." I pause. "Thank you for everything."

She opens her eyes. "What are you thanking me for?"

"For Hannah, for the boys I love as much as I love her, for loving me, for being you, and ..." I peck her lips, "for coming home in the first place. None of this would ever have happened if you hadn't made that decision."

"Best decision I've ever made." She kisses my chest.

"And for last night. Being with you while you gave birth was everything." I kiss her temple. "You gave me my heart back."

She raises her head. "What do you mean?"

"The minute you walked back into my life, I felt alive. It was like waking up after a long sleep."

Her lips twitch. "I'm not sure if you realise that you did the same for me. It might have taken me a while, but I got there. And I have no regrets."

She leans her head on my chest, and I close my eyes.

There are still days I can't quite believe my life. I was so sure that even if I found love again, I wouldn't have all I do now.

The boys have three parents as far as we're concerned, and my little girl is the icing on the cake.

I'm sure I'll be up in the night just to look and make sure she's still real.

And in my arms is the woman I'll spend the rest of my life treasuring, because I never thought I'd ever be the one who had Chloe's love.

I'll never take that for granted.

Beside the bed, I hear a tiny whimper, and I pull away from Chloe.

"Where are you going?" she asks.

"To check on the baby."

"The baby's fine."

"She made a noise."

Chloe laughs softly. "She'll make lots of little noises while she sleeps. If you're going to climb out of bed every time she snuffles, then I'll move her to her room."

I raise my eyebrows. "You're not taking my little girl anywhere."

"Then I'll sleep in the spare room and you can get up to her fifty times a night." She rolls over, and I reach for her, pulling her in tight. Chloe looks back over her shoulder. "Aren't you getting out of bed?"

"No. I'll stay put." I link my fingers in hers and rest our hands on her stomach. It takes me back to the first night we spent together—the night I realised she had feelings for me.

"Good." She yawns. "Let's get some sleep before she really does wake up. I'm not sure any of you are ready for what's to come."

I chuckle, kissing the back of her neck. She's probably right. I have no idea what's to come.

But I do know there's no way I could do this with anyone else.

Only ever Chloe.

ALSO BY WENDY SMITH

The Copper Creek Series

Coming Home

Doctor's Orders

Baker's Dozen

Hunter's Mark

Teacher's Pet

Fall and Rise Duet

Falling

Rising

Fall and Rise - The Complete Duet

The Aeon Series

Game On

Build a Nerd

Bar None

Coming soon Love on Site

Hollywood Kiwis Series

Common Ground

Even Ground

Under Ground

Coming soon Rocky Ground

Stand alones

For the Love of Chloe

Coming 2022 Lost and Found

The Friends Duet

Loving Rowan

Three Days

The Forever Series

Something Real

The Right One

Unexpected

Chances Series

Another Chance

Taking Chances

Lifetime Series

In a Lifetime

In an Instant

In a Heartbeat

In the End

At the Start

ABOUT THE AUTHOR

Wendy Smith published as Ariadne Wayne for three years before deciding she didn't want to be someone else all the time. She's an Apple Books and Nook bestselling author, whose book In the End, written as Ariadne Wayne, was named one of Apple's best books of 2017. All her stories come with a quirky sense of humour , and she cries over everything.

Find me online
www.wendysmith.co.nz
wendy@wendysmith.co.nz

www.ingramcontent.com/pod-product-compliance
Lightning Source LLC
Chambersburg PA
CBHW030134010826
48973CB00002B/560

* 9 7 8 1 9 9 1 3 0 3 0 2 8 *